UNITY ZONE

JOSUE FRANCOIS

authorHOUSE®

AuthorHouse™
1663 Liberty Drive
Bloomington, IN 47403
www.authorhouse.com
Phone: 1 (800) 839-8640

Published by AuthorHouse   10/01/2015

ISBN: 978-1-5049-5433-4 (sc)
ISBN: 978-1-5049-5432-7 (e)

T he Thunder Warriors go way back. Starting eight hundred thousand years ago, they began fighting the evil Omnizar. But this wasn't just any war. Omnizar wanted the sacred phoenix crystals—the deadliest power that has ever existed. The crystals could be used to summon the fire phoenix lightning dragon, a powerful creature that could destroy Omnizar and vanquish him back to hell. So he wanted to make sure that the Thunder Warriors no longer existed.

Surothion, who was the leader of the Thunder Warriors, wouldn't let Omnizar triumph; he decided to continue his quest as the leader of the Thunder Warriors. This was why, in the future, he would run into a group of college students—Billy, Kenneth, Larutio, Zomar, Randy, Letitia, Jennifer, and Cody. These young Thunder Warriors would encounter Surothion when he brought them together so they could help fight the evil vampires and demons Omnizar was sending. The eight young warriors didn't become friends until they were united during one morning when they were in school and Omnizar sent one of his demons to terrorize the people of Star Field City, Minnesota.

"Kenneth, you are always acting like being sensitive is very serious," said Cody.

"Dude, I'm not being too anxious. It's just that life is too serious for us to take it as a joke," said Kenneth.

"All right. I would like for everyone to open their books to page sixty-five. Billy, can you read for us?" said Professor Aaron.

"When mountains are presented before us, there are situations that we can't overcome, but having hope and courage will help us to get through the daily situations and emotional issues that will have an impact," read Billy.

"Thank you for reading for us. Okay, everybody, the lesson talks about overcoming fear—the fear of doing something positive. We all have this nervousness inside, but it's okay to not chicken out," said Professor Aaron.

"Professor Aaron, you have to understand, I'm still trying to knock out the possibility of having to be afraid of talking to people," said Larutio.

"Yeah, but you have to take a look at the other side. I'm not afraid of accomplishing anything. I'm just a defiant person," said Jennifer.

"Hey, I'm still the soldier I've always been, no matter what life brings me," said Zomar.

"On the board I am showing you guys a pattern of success. Once you take a closer look, you'll see how the pattern is broken down. First let me explain; you are born as a baby, then you grow up and go to school and get a degree. Once you have your degree, you'll find a job at a big company, and—boom!—everything changes," said Professor Aaron.

"You make it sound so funny and awesome. I guess the way you explained it is correct; that's how life is," said Randy.

"The lesson has ended, and everyone can close their books. I will be seeing all of you tomorrow when I give you your science project," said Professor Aaron.

"I'm just hoping that this science project will be totally awesome and cool," said Letitia.

After class was over, Kenneth, Billy, and Zomar, along with Jennifer, went to the Fusion Burger Shop. They were having lunch, but trouble was getting ready to take place. Omnizar stood right in front of them. He had summoned his demon, whose job was to terrorize people.

"Hello, Thunder Warriors. It is nice to see that four of you are having lunch together," said Omnizar.

"You've got no right to be here. Get out," said Kenneth.

"I'll go ahead and make the rest of your day interesting. I summoned Ricto. If you take a look outside, I believe that my demon is terrorizing those earth humans. Ha-ha! Farewell," said Omnizar as he departed.

"That was totally strange of Omnizar to pop in on us like that," said Billy.

"Hi, you guys! Welcome to the Fusion Burger Shop. May I take your order?" said Betty Ann.

"We would like to have cheeseburgers with side orders of fries and lava chocolate milk shakes," said Jennifer.

"Oh, don't forget to add two patties, so I can have a double burger to eat," said Kenneth.

"All of you can have a seat, and the chef will be making your meals. Don't worry; this will only take a couple of minutes," said Betty Ann.

"Guys, as crazy as it may sound, I just saw one of Omnizar's demons," said Zomar.

"Do you think that we'd better go? I certainly would not want to miss my meal," said Billy.

"We are going to have to teleport out of here, so Betty Ann doesn't see us," said Kenneth.

"You're right. We're out of here. Let's go," said Jennifer.

"I'm guessing that you Thunder Warriors have come to stop me," said Ricto.

"You're not going anywhere, Ricto, because we're here to destroy you," Thunder Striker Kenneth shouted.

"Ha-ha! Oh, please don't flatter yourselves, because that lightning you used only tickled me," Ricto said.

"Hey, that wasn't fair. It's like our lightning strikes were peanut butter toast," said Billy.

"Well, then, Thunder Warriors, this is it for all of you," shouted Ricto.

"Hold it right there. I've come to interrupt this fight. I'm getting all of you to safety right now. Peace out, Ricto," said Surothion.

When Surothion saved the Thunder Warriors from Omnizar's demon, he brought them to his lair so he could explain everything to them.

"Thank you for saving us. We don't know why you brought us here, though. Who are you?" asked Jennifer.

"I am the supreme leader of the Thunder Warriors," said Surothion.

"Wait, I've heard a lot about you. You're Surothion. When the war broke out eight hundred thousand years ago, you fought alongside our great relatives," said Jennifer.

"That's right. I'm surprised that your relatives gave up being Thunder Warriors and went to other cities," said Surothion.

"Wow, your memory is very bright. No one forgets anything that happened in the past," said Zomar.

"I know that all of you are just learning how to use your thunder powers, and I have to train you guys properly," said Surothion.

"Hey, you're right. We're just beginners. Maybe you will help us out," said Kenneth.

"It takes practice to become the best warriors. You guys always have to remember there are other people who are Thunder Warriors, and I'm going to get them now. Peace out," said Surothion.

Surothion went to fight Ricto, and he had help from four other Thunder Warriors, who hadn't been united with the other ones.

"I told you that I was going to return, and this would not be good for you," shouted Surothion, releasing a magnum thunder strike.

"No! Your attack has destroyed the indestructible shield that was protecting me," said Ricto.

"You were very foolish to think that some useless shield would stop my attack. Guess again," said Surothion.

"I see that you have some of your buddies with you. It doesn't matter. Shadow vampires will get them," said Ricto.

"Oh, no, you don't! Your vampires will never succeed. Surothion, let's split up," said Larutio.

"These shadow vampires won't even strike me," shouted Surothion as he produced a supreme lightning blaze.

"This can't be happening. Your attack has destroyed the vampires, including me," said Ricto.

"Tell Omnizar that one day he shall return to hell, which is where he came from," said Surothion.

After Surothion destroyed Ricto and the shadow vampires, he returned to his lair with the remaining Thunder Warriors. Meanwhile, Omnizar was planning his evil deeds so he could cause chaos.

"Zervo, I couldn't believe that Ricto was defeated by that damn Surothion, who is my greatest foe," said Omnizar.

"Master Omnizar, I propose that you send your acid virus to infect those earth humans. Ha-ha," said Zervo.

"That sounds like a great idea, so I'm going to get on board with it. Viral Tron, come forth," yelled Omnizar.

"You don't have anything to panic about, Master Omnizar. I will remain invisible, and the humans won't even know when they are being infected. Farewell," said Viral Tron.

Viral Tron went to earth, quickly turning invisible. The people were being injected, but they didn't know what was going on.

When they went to sleep, the only thing they felt was just some needles pinching them.

The Thunder Warriors began to sit down. Once Surothion had a conversation with them, he did his training.

"I've brought all of you here to become part of the Thunder Warriors team," said Surothion.

"I'm not quite sure that we should be part of the Thunder Warriors, since it is very extreme for us," said Cody.

"I'm trying to explain that we are a powerful force, and Omnizar is no match for any of us once we're united as a team," said Surothion.

"Being part of the thunder team means a lot. I'm honored to be fighting alongside all of you guys," said Jennifer.

"But, guys, all of us have to protect this city, since it is a part of our jobs," said Randy.

"I'm very disturbed by Omnizar wanting to destroy the people of this city," said Larutio.

"Look, I know that you guys don't have an understanding of how things are, but being a hero is very important. The city would never be able to live without you," said Surothion.

"Okay, we agree to be part of the Thunder Warriors team and help to fight crime," said Billy.

"All of you can go now. I wouldn't want anyone to be late for school, which begins in twenty-eight minutes," said Surothion.

The eight friends left Surothion's lair. They went to school so they would not miss their classes.

Viral Tron was on earth, and it was doing more damage than anyone could imagine, since it was chewing on humans' ears and vanquishing their bodies as the deadly virus destroyed them.

"Welcome back to class, guys. I see that all of you are exhausted," said Professor Aaron.

"Professor Aaron, coming here is just another day for us," said Cody.

"You're here to learn and to have a future. Your science project is about what comes from asteroids when they crash on the earth. This lesson will reveal a lot of mysteries to all of you. I'm ready to take questions starting now," said Professor Aaron.

"Professor, I believe that you can find diamonds inside asteroids—diamonds that are used to make jewelry," said Zomar.

"That is correct. I'm shocked that you know your stuff; I find it to be very amazing," said Professor Aaron.

"Everyone has to see the bright side of the asteroids. After all, they can cause holes in the center of the earth," said Jennifer.

"Sometimes I wonder what would happen if an asteroid had a virus that could cause us to become sick," said Kenneth.

"Dude, that will never happen; besides, we would become extinct and not exist," said Billy.

"I get what you are saying. I was just furious about not getting to see beyond outer space," said Kenneth.

"I'm not finished yet. We were digging deep into space. There is a black hole hidden in outer space. If it comes to earth, then we are all doomed," said Professor Aaron.

"There are a lot of astronauts who try to find the mysteries of space, but they never have any luck," said Letitia.

"The only thing I can say is that we don't know too much about the galaxy. Every single clue will never be revealed to us," said Cody.

"Now we are getting to the interesting part. There are billions of stars in space. Atomic matter breaks down the cosmic energy and fuses together and forms these rock particles, which become a meteor shower that crashes into the earth," said Professor Aaron.

"Whoa, you are teaching us a lot about meteor showers. Maybe it will help us to become better at our studies," said Jennifer.

"I also have a video that I'm going to be showing all of you. Just watch and learn, and everything will be all right. I used to be an astronomer," said Professor Timothy.

"Ay, I could've sworn that I just felt somebody injecting me with a shot in my left arm," said Lynx.

"Maybe you are just exaggerating; it could've been an insect bite," said Ashley.

"I know what I felt, and I've got the scars to prove it. Here," said Lynx, extending her arm.

"Whoa. I suggest that you go to the doctor's office and get an examination," said Randy.

"No more talking, please. Just watch the video; maybe it will help you to pass tomorrow's test," said Professor Aaron.

"I apologize, Professor Aaron, but somebody had a problem. I think that you'd better talk to them," said Cody.

"I will do that now. Oh no, Lynx, she just fell to the ground and collapsed. Somebody call an ambulance," said Professor Aaron.

"Help me; my voice is gone, and I can't speak anymore," said Lynx.

"Oh no. She's vaporizing into dust. I don't know what to do," said Professor Aaron.

"The best option that you have is to end this lesson now before she dies," said Billy.

"All right. The lesson has ended, and all of you can go home. I will stay right here with her until the ambulance comes," said Professor Aaron.

"How is she doing so far? It's a good thing that we made it in time," said the EMS worker.

"Her vital signs are starting to fail, and she's not showing too much pulse," said Professor Aaron.

"We are going to do some blood tests on her and hope that she will get better," said the EMS worker.

Since class had ended, Kenneth and his friends went to his house. They sat down and planned how they were going to stop Viral Tron from destroying the people of Minnesota.

"We need to break down our battle plan in order to destroy Viral Tron," said Randy.

"There is a huge problem. Viral Tron can't be tracked because he is moving rapidly from person to person. We don't know when he will make his next move," said Billy.

"I've laid out a map of hunting. First we will turn invisible, and then we'll destroy Viral Tron with our lightning attacks," said Zomar.

"Dude, you need to put that map away. We must try to be heroic and courageous," said Cody.

"If we can't come up with a decision, then I suppose all of us will have to do this all over again," said Jennifer.

"Hold on a minute. I have to step in now. Do you mean to tell me that we're going to let Viral Tron wreak havoc and not take action?" asked Larutio.

"The best option we've got is for Surothion to help us out now," said Letitia.

"I heard you call my name as I was getting ready to come here," said Surothion.

"Boss, we can't come up with an attack plan that will work for all of us," said Kenneth.

"This is not about you having an attack plan. Besides, I'm the leader; no one put you in charge of this team," said Surothion.

"Okay, then, we will do things your way," said Zomar.

"We shall remain invisible so the humans don't see us fighting Viral Tron and expect us to succeed," said Surothion.

The Thunder Warriors turned invisible, and they went with Surothion to help fight Viral Tron. They caught Viral Tron inside a girl's room; she was sleeping when Viral Tron snuck up on her.

"Hey, Viral Tron, enough of this madness. We won't let you continue to do any more of this evil," said Surothion.

"If it isn't the mighty Surothion. I'm sure that you will never get close to me. I've got a trick for you; try to figure out which one is the real me," said Viral Tron.

"Viral Tron has made it more complicated for us since he has made multiple copy clones of himself," said Larutio.

"And there is another thing. I didn't forget the shadow vampires. You'll have to get all them too," said Viral Tron.

"We are now fighting an army. This should be cool," Cody shouted.

"All of you shouldn't be so sure that I'm here. Besides, I already left; I'm at Omnizar's lair," said Viral Tron.

"Damn! I should've known that this was a trick all along. I felt like we were vanquishing," said Jennifer.

"I feel very sorry for you Thunder Warriors because you've been banished to the viral Rx dimension," said Zenox.

"Take care of yourself, Surothion. We're going away; please promise us that you will find a way to set us free," said Billy.

"Don't be afraid, Billy. I'll figure out how to get you out of the Rx dimension," said Surothion.

"Surothion, you're the only one left. I suppose you don't want to fight any of us," said Ingo.

"I guarantee you that I will be back with shadow vampires. Farewell for now," said Surothion.

The Thunder Warriors were defeated and banished to the viral dimension. They knew that it wasn't going to be easy for them to be freed from that dimension, but Surothion stepped in to help out and everything was going to change.

"I can't believe this. It feels like we've become total failures," said Kenneth.

"Come on, now. Don't blame yourself. This should be on all of us. I never knew that Viral Tron has his own virus network dimension," said Zomar.

"You see, this is exactly what I'm talking about. It was a trap all along, and we fell for it," said Randy.

"Something is very fishy about the Rx dimension; it feels like our thunder powers are being drained and destroyed," said Letitia.

"You're right. I'm starting to lose consciousness and can't get up from the floor of this dimension," said Larutio.

"Remember what Surothion told us: giving up is never the option because we stand united as the Thunder Warriors," said Cody.

"Hey, you're right. Whoa! You guys need to look above you; I see Surothion coming," said Kenneth.

"I hope I didn't miss the party; it wouldn't be fun without me," said Surothion.

"It is such a relief that you came to save us, or death would've been knocking in our faces," said Billy.

"I want all of you to hold hands tight. I've done this before. Crimson lightning orb, activate," said Surothion.

"Whoa, I feel totally different now since the lightning portal has reenergized us," said Larutio.

"Things are about to change. The fight with Viral Tron was not anything it appeared to be. We will have to do much better," said Surothion.

After Surothion saved the Thunder Warriors from Viral Tron's Rx dimension, they went to his lair. He was very serious about them becoming better fighters. Surothion started the long-awaited training.

"Some of you haven't become the fighters that you claim to be, so I will show you how to use your skills to apprehend and destroy the opponent. All of you will be fighting me at the same time to test which moves are your weaknesses. We will begin now. I'm turning the place into a holographic training room. Let's go," said Surothion.

"So, this is it, huh? You better move aside, tall giant," Thunder Striker Kenneth shouted.

"Nice swing, Kenneth, but remember Surothion has the upper hand. Ooh, he just body-slammed you on your neck," Thunder Maze Billy shouted.

"I've got something for you, Billy boy—a supreme lightning blaze," shouted Surothion.

"Ay, your thunder attack is more powerful than mine," said Billy.

"That's because I'm the best warrior you've ever seen; my father trained me very well," said Surothion.

"Billy, dude, you are such an idiot. Surothion's attack knocked you twenty-five feet into that pit," said Randy.

"Hey, it's not my fault. I tried, but he was moving too quick," said Billy.

"I am very impressed with you, Surothion. You've already defeated Billy and Kenneth. I'm certain that you won't be able to reflect my attack," Lightning Obliterator Randy shouted.

"Ay, your attack is too strong, and I will reflect it with my crimson futon," said Surothion.

"No way! This is insane. Your attack has completely paralyzed me. I give up," said Randy.

"Somebody has to step their game up. You've already beaten three of the guys, and I'm the fourth one," Imperial Lightning Destroyer Zomar shouted.

"Since you are the fourth one, I'm going to knock you out cold to the ground. I don't mind breaking my knuckles for this," Supreme Lightning Blaze Surothion shouted.

"You guys are such losers. As I'm watching you fight Surothion, his attacks are blowing you away one by one. I surely won't be defeated by him," Lamecnia's Thunder Larutio shouted.

"You shall suffer the same fate your buddies did," shouted Supreme Lightning Blaze Surothion.

"I can't feel my body, and your attack has injured me," said Larutio.

"I already warned you, Larutio, that I'm not someone you'll beat that easily," said Surothion.

"What is going on here? It's like the powerful one can't be defeated by those guys. It's my turn," Imperial Thunder Cody shouted.

"Cody, you are too young to understand the meaning of power, so I suggest you take some karate classes," shouted Supreme Lightning Blaze Surothion.

"Whoa, I've lost control of my energy, and I can't use my strength," said Cody.

"I only confused your thunder powers. When the time comes for you to have a battle, you will be ready," said Surothion.

"I am shocked that Surothion would do that kind of damage. He showed you guys the real meaning of a true warrior," said Jennifer.

"You're just a girl that doesn't have the chops to beat me in this training," said Surothion.

"Hey, I'll show you who's a girl," Surenolize Thunder Jennifer shouted.

"Ooh, that attack just made me want to have a crush on you—just kidding," shouted Supreme Lightning Blaze Surothion.

"Oh, I just hit my head on the wall since your attack knocked me out so hard," said Jennifer.

"You should be thankful that I didn't hurt you too badly," said Surothion.

"Well, I'm okay, but next time it will be different when we fight," said Jennifer.

"I guess it's my turn, and I won't let you do to me what you just did to Jennifer," Circon Thunder Letitia shouted.

"Fighting a girl is like me riding a horse that goes to the farm," shouted Supreme Lightning Blaze Surothion.

"Isn't there anyone that could beat Surothion?" said Jennifer.

"Jennifer, do not be afraid. I'm the eighth person that's going to fight Surothion, and believe me, it's going to be a draw," said Larutio.

"Watch out! Surothion is tall and powerful. He will do the same thing to you that he did to us," said Jennifer.

"I'm not even concerned about Surothion. Once we fight, it's going to be a draw," said Larutio.

"You should've turned back and went home to your mommy," said Surothion.

"I've got no reason to go home since I'm here to prove that I am the best fighter," said Larutio.

"You haven't quite gotten up to my level yet, but we shall see," shouted Supreme Lightning Blaze Surothion.

"You've underestimated me, Surothion, so I'll even the odds up," Proton Lightning Fury Larutio shouted.

"No, I absolutely can't believe this! Your attack is pushing mine away and we're locked in a clash," said Surothion.

"That's what you get for thinking that no one else is superior to you," said Larutio.

"Dude, I will never let you win. I'm the best of the best, and that is why my attack is pushing harder toward yours," said Surothion.

"You are too powerful, but I'm stronger than you," said Larutio.

"As you can see, this battle was a draw since our attacks knocked both of us very hard against the wall," said Surothion.

"I know what you are saying, and this fight was the coolest one," said Larutio.

"All right, guys. Your training is over, and everybody did very well. I'm going to let all of you go now, and later on I will be working on a cure so the people don't die from this acid virus that Viral Tron injected them with," said Surothion.

"We had such a wonderful time! See you later, head boss," said Cody.

The eight Thunder Warriors left Surothion's lair and went to school. But tonight something terrible was going to happen: there was a meteor shower that was going to take place. The Thunder Warriors would be knocked out cold by this meteor shower; they would feel their powers completely gone. Surothion was going to be the only one that retained his thunder powers.

"You guys don't know how happy I am to teach you about Mother Nature. This lesson will certainly have you interested in the weather," said Professor Aaron.

"Professor Aaron, I wanted to ask you about Lynx and how she is doing," said Zomar.

"Lynx is doing very well. The doctors gave her some antibiotics, and she is getting better. They told me she is stable day by day. I hope she has a good recovery so she can come back to school," said Professor Aaron.

"That's good to hear. I can't wait to see her once she comes back. We will have 'get well' cards for her," said Zomar.

"We all know that Mother Nature always has its impact all over the world, but today I'm showing you that Mother Nature can cause us to lose control of ourselves," said Professor Aaron.

"I've always noticed that once we get a hurricane boom, everything is left in ruins, and the city has been completely destroyed," said Kenneth.

"Dude, you have to remember that these are natural disasters that happen every year, and we need to be very careful or one of us will end up dead," said Billy.

"The main thing that kills me about these disasters is that people are unprepared and they don't have time to run away and get to safety," said Jennifer.

"The reason why we have these terrible disasters is that global warming is reaching its peak of the chain. Every year it's becoming a lot colder than it was. The reason that we have global warming is that the oil companies are drilling too many holes into the ground," said Professor Aaron.

"My problem is that the factories are releasing chemicals into the air that are making everyone sick," said Randy.

"When it snows we always feel these gusts of strong winds blowing toward us, which I think is very dangerous, but hey, that's how the weather has been since the beginning of time," said Letitia.

"New Jersey gets hit with high floods. Since I've done my research, I know that a basement is unsafe for people to live in. Pay attention, everyone. I'm showing you a map of the fifty states. We are in the same category as these other thirty-eight states, which are the worst places to live in," said Professor Aaron.

"You have to examine the facts. Slumlords exist everywhere. We just need to find a clean space that doesn't have any rats," said Thomas.

"I've got a book of pictures here. Take it and pass them around. You will see the damages that have been caused by some of the worst disasters," said Professor Aaron.

"Whoa, I can't bear to look at these pictures; these damages look so horrific," said Larutio.

"Now you see that natural disasters cost 68 billion dollars in damages. The last hurricane we had was back in 2008, and forty-five people were killed," said Professor Aaron.

"I just felt a sudden heaviness under my eyes," said Mack.

"Sometimes we all feel heaviness under our eyes; just don't worry about it. Tomorrow I will be giving everyone a quiz, so bring your pens and do the best you can. The lesson is over; peace out," said Professor Aaron.

"That was a very long lesson. For the entire time, my head was flat on the desk," said Jennifer.

"I really didn't care about the lesson being long. Now come on, it's just school," said Kenneth.

"The sun is starting to go away quickly. I find it very weird that it is dark at one o'clock in the afternoon," said Billy.

"There's a meteor shower taking place right now," said Randy.

"Guys, I was thinking that we should stand here and watch the meteor shower," said Cody.

"I guess we've got time to see something extreme," said Larutio.

"Wow, this meteor shower looks very nice. I could just have a seat and sit back," said Zomar.

"Ay, I can't move; this meteor shower is taking away our energy," said Letitia.

"You're not the only one that's dying. Somebody help us," said Billy.

"The meteor shower has us chained to the ground in circles, and my body has become very weak," said Kenneth.

"I never thought that this would happen. In five years we're losing and Omnizar is winning," said Randy.

"This meteor shower is taking everything that we once had, and the people won't be able to defend themselves," said Jennifer.

"My soul is almost gone. Surothion, help us wherever you are," said Zomar.

"I'm coming, guys. Don't be afraid; I'm right here," said Surothion.

"We're going to need you to pull us out now," said Billy.

Surothion teleported back to his lair with the eight Thunder Warriors because the meteor shower did a lot of damage to them; their thunder powers were gone. Surothion was going to figure out a way to help them get their powers back, but he had a lot of work on his hands to do. Meanwhile Omnizar sent Viral Tron to continue his chaos spree; Omnizar was celebrating the end of the Thunder Warriors.

"Zervo, this is perfect. I feel like we are approaching a new day because those Thunder Warriors don't have their powers anymore," said Omnizar.

"Master Omnizar, it couldn't be better without you envisioning the destruction of those Thunder Warriors," said Zervo.

"Viral Tron, I know that it is only nighttime and I'm sending you back to earth so you can continue your terror," said Omnizar.

"I will be very delighted to go. Good-bye, Master Omnizar," said Viral Tron.

Viral Tron went back to earth. He had turned the planet into a cybernetwork, but this wasn't just any cybernetwork. It had virus wires that looked like a dome, and it covered the entire planet. The people of Battle Dome City felt a lot of cyberattacks on their computers, and they saw a message on their monitor screens that said, "Tomorrow the earth would be terminated." Everyone felt their bodies turning into viral computer messages, and this was very crazy. Viral Tron sat on a chair and was laughing. Meanwhile, Surothion was going to restore the powers that the Thunder Warriors had lost, but he couldn't keep waiting a lot longer.

"We're too weak to even speak. Do you have a drink of water for me?" said Kenneth.

"Here you go. The cup is right next to your head, and it has a lot of water," said Surothion.

"Thanks a lot. I feel refreshed now," said Kenneth.

"Surothion, you are like a father to us. We appreciate that you always look out for us," said Billy.

"I can't say too much. But the only thing I do have to tell you is to sit back; there is something explosive coming. I have to tell all of you … do you remember the virus that Viral Tron infected people with? The only way to set them free is to destroy Viral Tron," said Surothion.

"I see that you've got us attached to some machine. How is that supposed to help?" asked Jennifer.

"This is my power restoration machine. As you can clearly see, the powers that all of you lost will be given back to you, but this may take four hours," said Surothion.

"We can't wait that long since Viral Tron is outside vanquishing the people," said Larutio.

"I demand that all of you have patience. Everything takes time. It's not like you're going to be like, 'Oh, I'm ready to fight now,'" said Surothion.

"Whoa, I feel the power returning inside me. Surothion, you've got another problem to be worried about: those meteor rocks won't wipe out your powers too, will they?" asked Cody.

"I've got nothing to be worried about. The meteor rocks can't affect me since my powers are unstoppable," said Surothion.

"Whoa, I think it's incredible the meteor rocks won't injure you at all," said Jennifer.

"I might have to leave you guys here until you're finished getting your powers back," said Surothion.

"You can stop being so panicky about us. We're fine, and we'll see you later," said Randy.

Surothion went to fight Viral Tron as the Thunder Warriors regenerated at his lair, but Viral Tron wasn't going to make this an easy fight. He used every possible trick that he could, and Surothion was going to find out that Viral Tron was more powerful than he thought.

"Surothion, it is very foolish of you to come and fight me alone," said Viral Tron.

"I'm never scared to be bold and fight others who can't win," said Surothion.

"I have just noticed something: the Thunder Warriors aren't around," said Viral Tron.

"They are in a safe place that's returning their powers to them," said Surothion.

"You should've abandoned this fight, since Master Omnizar is going to succeed. Ha-ha," said Viral Tron.

"I refuse to surrender to evil because that will never happen," Supreme Lightning Blaze Surothion shouted.

"I see that you are using your lightning attacks, so I'll summon my virecs to come forth and destroy you," said Viral Tron.

"Surothion, we're sorry to disappoint you, but we've got our virus protection shield, which protects us from any lightning attacks," said the virecs when they arrived.

"If you're going to be using some kind of rubber shield, I suggest you bring it on," shouted Surothion.

"Ay, you've destroyed our shield. It doesn't matter, though; your life is over," shouted the virecs.

"Viral Tron is going to regret that he ever did any of this madness," shouted Surothion.

"This wasn't supposed to happen. You destroyed my virecs, and now I guess it's just you and me. Bring it on, Surothion," said Viral Tron.

"I really didn't like how your virecs talked trash, but hey, they proved to be no match for me," said Surothion.

"You're just a flatterer who doesn't know when to quit," shouted Viral Tron.

"Oh, please, you're just jealous that I'm the supreme soldier that has the upper hand," shouted Surothion.

The attack that came from Surothion destroyed Viral Tron, and the earth was returned to normal. So were the people. The virus infections were gone, and so was Viral Tron's viral network. The sun was getting ready to come up after the fight. Surothion left and returned to the lair so he could see how the Thunder Warriors were doing.

"I see that you guys have left the restoration machines. Are all of you feeling better?" asked Surothion.

"We feel like we've just left another planet from space," said Zomar.

"I'm very happy to hear that. I couldn't bear to lose any of you to a tragedy," said Surothion.

"Look, I know that we are very important to you and the world, so everything should be all right," said Randy.

"I guess we're leaving now. We have to go home and get ready for school. I had such a great sleep, and that machine of yours was very comfortable," said Cody.

"See you guys later, and have a great afternoon," said Surothion.

"You take care of yourself, boss," said Letitia.

The eight Thunder Warriors left Surothion's lair. They went home, but there would be a problem. Each and every one of them would have been late for school, but Larutio hurried up and gave everybody a ride to school before the bell rang.

"Where have you guys been? Class started ten minutes ago," said Professor Aaron.

"I can explain. There was an emergency in the family, and we had to go to the hospital," said Billy.

"That's not how everyone saw it happen. A lot of people told me that you guys were chained to the ground by the meteor rocks that came from the sky," said Professor Aaron.

"I think it's completely crazy to think we were chained to the ground; me and my friends were just in a hurry," said Randy.

"I will not continue to have this conversation with you anymore. I waited seven minutes for you guys to get here. I'm giving you the test papers. Pass them around and take one each," said Professor Aaron.

"Wow, I'm stunned that this quiz is one hundred questions long," said Cody.

"The quiz is about everything I've taught for the last two days. Use your brain to focus and not wander somewhere else," said Professor Timothy.

"Professor, I'm going to use my head to do this test since I remember all of the answers," said Jennifer.

"Would you just be silent. I want everyone to close their mouths. No talking during a quiz, or you will be given an F-plus," said Professor Aaron.

"Larutio, I guess we can speak through our minds, and Professor Aaron won't hear us," said Zomar.

"I have to tell you that this test is too damn easy for me," said Larutio.

"I'm not even concerned at all. Besides, we're intelligent ones who can pass anything," said Zomar.

"If you are done, come up and hand me your test so I can grade it right now," said Professor Aaron.

"Here you go. I'm all finished, Professor Aaron. This test was just a piece of cake for me," said Kenneth.

After the eight friends finished their school quiz, they went to the park so they could play some basketball so their day would be fun.

"I'm thinking about playing some basketball. Are you guys with me?" said Billy.

"Dude, I will crush in a game of street, but check it out; it will be three on three," said Randy.

"Me and Letitia will sit down and watch you guys play just for the fun of it," said Jennifer.

"Larutio, pass me the ball so I can do my killer slam dunk," said Zomar.

"Here you go, buddy. You better fly over their heads," said Larutio.

"Yes, I did, and that is one point and zero for you, Billy," said Zomar.

"I suggest you move aside since I'm rolling in circles; I'll shoot a three-pointer," said Billy.

"You should've been on the sideline to stop Billy from making that three-pointer, Randy. What is wrong with you, dude?" said Kenneth.

"Look, it's not my fault. I tried my hardest to move quickly; I guess I wasn't fast enough," said Randy.

"Jennifer, these guys play ball like they are in the NBA," said Letitia.

"Well, you know how they have always been. You certainly can't blame them," said Jennifer.

"Time out. I'm too tired to play, and we need a break now," said Randy.

"Do you give, because we've kicked your butt?" said Kenneth.

"I quit, and you guys win because playing basketball is too much work for me," said Randy.

"You didn't even do that much. You mean to tell me that passing the ball caused you to be exhausted?" asked Larutio.

"I kind of hit my knee, so we're done for now," said Billy.

"You're just a quitter. Come on. It wasn't like you were trying enough to beat us," said Zomar.

"Ladies, did you two enjoy watching the game?" asked Cody.

"We were just laughing and giggling and telling some jokes. The game was all right, but promise me you won't rough each other up next time," said Jennifer.

"It was very hectic since you guys are good people," said Letitia.

After the eight friends finished playing basketball, they went home since it had been a long day. Darkness was hovering over the sun, and daylight didn't happen until the end of the week.

The Thunder Warriors were trying to find out what was causing this. They didn't know that Omnizar was causing this because he wanted to take away the sunlight. The animals began to die when the darkness caused them to get burned by solar ray beams that came from the stars.

"Jennifer, just please settle down since we've got another emergency," said Kenneth.

"Don't you think that the people of Star Field City might die from no sunlight?" said Jennifer.

"Not having sunlight for a couple of days can't be that bad if the person is on an oxygen machine," said Billy.

"I'm so worried right now that it isn't even a joke. What if the people get hit with burning stars from space?" asked Cody.

"All of you must calm down, or you're going to lose your minds," said Surothion.

"You're right. Maybe we're overreacting and shouldn't take it so serious," said Randy.

"Omnizar is behind all of this. He is using his crystal rods, and we must destroy those rods now," said Surothion.

"Surothion, I've picked up some stuff. There are solar ray beams coming from space," said Cody.

"I can't sit here and not fight back. We must go and find those rods before it's too late," said Letitia.

"I've found the location of the crystal rods. They are in a field that looks like the Grand Canyon," said Surothion.

"Then let's go. I wouldn't want to see any sadness brought to the farmers," said Zomar.

The Thunder Warriors and Surothion went to the field that looked like the Grand Canyon, but Omnizar was getting ready to energize the crystal rods so he could create a giant hole in the center of the earth.

"Zervo, I see that Surothion is going to destroy my crystal rods, so I'll use everything I can to stop him," said Omnizar.

"Master Omnizar, you shouldn't let Surothion get to you. Destroy the infamous leader of the Thunder Warriors," said Zervo.

"You make a great point. I'll start by doing this dark shadow phantom orb energy releaser. Once the solar ray beams reflect at the crystal rods, they will see my demon come out of the ground," laughed Omnizar.

As Surothion and the Thunder Warriors arrived at the field that looked like the Grand Canyon, they saw the crystal rods were connected to the ground. As they attempted to destroy the crystal rods with their thunder powers, this didn't work because the solar ray beams that Omnizar sent to blow a large hole in the ground were going to make their way to the Grand Canyon–like field. But when this happened, they saw Zaroc, an ox demon, coming from the ground, and they were getting ready to fight it.

"Oh no, this is getting out of control. We tried to destroy the crystal rods, but it was too late," said Kenneth.

"You Thunder Warriors need to move aside," said Zaroc.

"Hey, we didn't see that one coming," said Billy.

"Master Omnizar has sent me to obliterate all of you, so if anyone wants a piece of me, bring it," said Zaroc.

"So, if you're not destroyed, then we won't see any sunlight? That's never going to happen; the light will shine," Supreme Lightning Blaze Surothion shouted.

"Ay, your attack just ripped off a piece of my horns, so I'll annihilate you," Zaru Destroyer Zaroc shouted.

"Hold it; our leader isn't fighting alone. We're in it together," Proton Lightning Fury Larutio shouted.

"He's right; we're not going to bow down to you," Imperial Thunder Cody shouted.

"All of you need to pause for a couple of minutes and listen. If you combine all of your lightning attacks with mine, then it should be enough," said Surothion.

"All right, guys, let's give our attacks to Surothion," Thunder Striker Kenneth shouted.

"Zirconium lightning fury," shouted Billy.

"Neutron lightning," shouted Zomar.

"Proton lightning," shouted Randy.

"Atomic thunder," shouted Cody.

"Astro lightning obliterator," shouted Larutio.

"Ravcon lightning," shouted Jennifer.

"Mercury lightning fury," shouted Letitia.

"What is going on here? You Thunder Warriors are powering up Surothion—it can't be," Zaru Destroyer Zaroc shouted.

"Zaroc, you lose. This is the end of the line for you," shouted Supreme Lightning Blaze Surothion.

The attacks that were used to power up Surothion destroyed Zaroc, and the sunlight came up. The Thunder Warriors were soon going to learn about the six dark witches that were vanquished into the phantom realm. This wasn't just another mystery; the witches posed a threat to the Thunder Warriors. Omnizar would soon bring them back, and this was going to cause chaos and destruction in Minnesota.

"We are really getting the hang of this. Zaroc was too simple for us," said Billy.

"Don't get too excited yet. When Omnizar sees that you're beating his demons, very soon he is going to make it tough for you," said Surothion.

"Surothion, I feel like some kind of evil force is trying to reach out to me," said Randy.

"Those witches are trying to find a vessel so they can come and conquer the earth," said Surothion.

"What do you mean by witches? Is there another enemy that we haven't fought yet?" asked Jennifer.

"This happened ten million years ago. A group of dark witches were trying to capture the earth and destroy the people, but the sacred wizards would not let it happen; they teamed up and imprisoned the witches within the phantom realm," said Surothion.

"Omnizar is always one step ahead of us. Do you think that he is trying to get his hands on the celestial medallions?" asked Zomar.

"There are seven medallions and a phoenix necklace that have been scattered throughout Minnesota; I believe that Omnizar will be sending his shadow vampires to hunt for them," said Surothion.

"Surothion, we will try to safeguard the seven medallions later on," said Letitia.

"I don't have a clue where the medallions are, but my powers should reveal the location once they are tracked down," said Surothion.

"Good-bye and take care," said Larutio.

The Thunder Warriors left Surothion's lair. They went on a scavenger hunt in the Minnesota mountains. They saw a ghost that looked like one of the witches, but they didn't bother going after her because a fog was looming all over the mountains.

"Oh, man, this is too much fog. How are we supposed to see?" asked Randy.

"Dude, I believe that the heat wave is causing all of this fog. We have to keep going until we find the treasure," said Billy.

"I saw something looking at us. It looked like a lady who had scars and shadow eyes, wearing a blue dress," said Zomar.

Just then he was interrupted by the witch, who said, "You Thunder Warriors, ha-ha, are setting foot in the wrong territory. No one has ever left these mountains alive."

"Hey, don't even try to cause the group to panic because your words don't scare any of us," said Larutio.

"Is that so? Well, good luck trying to get out of here. Farewell," said the witch.

"This is very strange. This sign is covered. Why don't I just remove it?" said Billy.

"Ay, we're trapped! The sign says the 'Mountain of No Return,'" said Letitia.

"Will everybody just stay calm? I think that the witch was just trying to scare us so we could be scaredy-cats," said Cody.

"Okay. This is very awkward. The ground under us is collapsing. Hold on to each other's hands so we don't get lost," said Kenneth.

"Larutio, I'm losing grip since the hole we're falling into is too deep," said Jennifer.

Moments later after they had all fallen through the hole, Randy said, "Whoa, we've finally landed on the ground. Did anyone get hurt? Are you guys all right?"

"I sense that this is the cave that has those medallions we're looking for," said Cody.

"Are you so sure? I don't see any medallions," said Billy.

"Well, we have to go to that narrow door at the end of this tunnel; the path looks very long," said Zomar.

"Do any of you have a flashlight? Or we will be walking in the dark," said Larutio.

"Don't worry. I've got one, and it's right here for us to use," said Cody.

"That feels much better. Now, how come we are seeing all of these dark seals on the walls of the cave?" asked Billy.

"The seals symbolize hidden traps we must watch out for," said Randy.

"This better not be one of those horror moments where a zombie jumps out from the walls and tries to eat us," said Jennifer.

"Stop talking all of that nonsense. There's no such thing as a zombie; that's just the movies," said Letitia.

"A strange thing just happened. My feet got caught in a rope, and I'm hanging upside down," said Kenneth.

"That's not a rope. Oh my god, a snake has you wrapped up. Whatever you do, don't move," said Billy.

"I refuse to let this snake eat me alive," shouted Thunder Striker Kenneth.

"At least that worked. Your attack blew the cobra away, and it slithered off," said Zomar.

"Now we can keep moving toward that iron door," said Cody.

"I don't feel comfortable getting closer to the door since it is opening up by itself," said Larutio.

"Whoa, did you feel that someone quickly pushed us inside this room? The door closed, and we're locked in for good," said Jennifer.

"All of you aren't going anywhere. Before you get the seven medallions, you must fight me," said Izon.

"We've always had an obstacle in front of us, but Izon is a dragon knight," said Kenneth.

"He is too tall for us to fight. We'd better run away now," said Billy.

"The eight of you claim to be Thunder Warriors, but when someone else is more powerful than you, the odds are totally different," said Izon.

"We are the ones that will defeat you with honor and dignity," shouted Lightning Obliterator Randy.

"Proton lightning fury," shouted Billy.

"Your attacks are powerful; they pack quite a punch," shouted Ariel Sword Neutron Fury Izon.

"Ay, Izon's attack is too strong; our attacks only reenergized him," said Randy.

"Are you guys fine? We don't know what else to do," said Zomar.

"Izon, we are asking you to please hand over the seven medallions so we can go already," said Cody.

"No, I'm not giving the seven medallions to anybody. If I do, then the six witches will be free to destroy the earth," said Izon.

"Have you ever heard of Surothion? He is our leader. If we don't get the medallions to him, then Omnizar will find them so he can cause chaos upon the earth," said Larutio.

"I know Surothion. You should've told me that you were working with him," said Izon.

"I'm sorry, but I thought that you were on the side of evil," said Jennifer.

"I would never support the forces of darkness since I represent those who do good," said Izon.

"I'm going to have to interrupt all of you. Izon, the medallions have to stay with me," said Surothion, who had just appeared.

"You can have them. I'll bring them to your lair now," said Izon.

"You can come, and thank you for giving the medallions to me. We're out of here," said Surothion.

Surothion and the Thunder Warriors left the tunnel that had the hidden medallions. Izon agreed to fight on their side since he was good friends with Surothion, so they all went to his lair. But Surothion was very mad at the Thunder Warriors since they didn't tell him that they were going to the caves that were hidden within the mountains.

"The eight of you could've gotten killed if I hadn't stepped in," said Surothion.

"I know that you really care about us, but hey, we were just doing our job. I certainly don't trust those mountains," said Kenneth.

"The only advice I'm going to give is that next time when you are going on an explosive adventure, tell me so I could be there to help out," said Surothion.

"You're not our father, and you can't tell us where we can't go. Guys, we're out of here," said Zomar.

"I am asking nicely, do not do anything that will put you in any danger for the rest of this day," said Surothion.

"We get it, and farewell. I'm also returning to my lair. Peace out," said Izon.

The eight friends left Surothion's lair. They were on their way home, but Omnizar had other plans for them.

"Oh man, sometimes Surothion talks to us so hard; I don't understand that," said Billy.

"Dude, he was just worried about our safety, and I agree that we should be careful in where we go," said Larutio.

"I get the point, but I don't like people talking to me like they own me," said Randy.

"We've got bigger fish to fry. Look, Omnizar is in front of us, and this is trouble," said Jennifer.

"You Thunder Warriors aren't going to make it home today," said Omnizar.

"You can't come here and threaten us. Stop the car, Kenneth, so we can get out and fight him," said Letitia.

"I'm unable to do that since we're in the middle of traffic," said Kenneth.

"I've got something for all of you—a dark shadow containment chain," shouted Omnizar.

"This is insane. Omnizar has wrapped us with shadow chains and ropes," said Cody.

"Kenneth, you and Billy are coming with me," said Omnizar.

"Yes, Master Omnizar. We shall obey your orders and do everything you tell us," said Kenneth.

Omnizar took Kenneth and Billy to his dimension. He was planning to brainwash them so he could get the medallions in order to release the six witches. The other Thunder Warriors were free after Omnizar left.

"Zervo, this is perfect. I've got two of the Thunder Warriors on our side now, so the other ones shouldn't be invincible at all. Ha-ha," said Omnizar.

"Master Omnizar, you are just so clever. I will never know how you do it; I won't ask you for an explanation," said Zervo.

"You need to take a closer look. The two Thunder Warriors are tied to my chair; they are being brainwashed by my machine," said Omnizar.

"You have to remember that their memories can't come back, or this will be a problem for us," said Zervo.

"Master Omnizar, the machine is hurting us," said Billy.

"It's okay, Billy. The machine will make your mind smarter," said Omnizar.

"Zervo, my device is rewiring their brains, and the name Surothion will never come out of their mouths," said Omnizar.

"You must find a way to trick Surothion so you get those damn medallions," said Zervo.

"I will be sending the two of them, and they will be playing like they are innocent," said Omnizar.

"I suspect that Surothion will be trying to send you back to hell, but he'd better get ready for the greatest fight ever," said Zervo.

"He's not strong enough to do it because the phoenix crystals haven't been found yet, and I sense that it will take him a while to do it," said Omnizar.

"Master Omnizar, stop the machine. We are ready to do your bidding," said Billy.

"This is excellent. I'm sending you back to earth. Go to Surothion's lair and pretend that you are back on his side; then bring me the medallions once and for all," said Omnizar.

"It shall be done; we won't disappoint you. Farewell," said Kenneth.

"One more thing—Surothion won't know what hit him. Ha-ha," said Billy.

Kenneth and Billy went to Surothion's lair. "I'm so happy that you guys are back. Did Omnizar hurt you in any way?" asked Jennifer.

"Nope. He didn't do anything bad to us. You guys need to give us the medallions," said Kenneth.

"The medallions are inside the desk drawer. You guys better keep them safe," said Larutio.

"You don't have anything to worry about. I will put them inside the treasure box that is inside my room," said Billy.

"We have to go since our families are having a barbecue," said Kenneth.

"We will be seeing you guys later, and take care," said Randy.

"Same thing for you, buddy. Peace out," said Billy.

When Surothion woke up, the Thunder Warriors told him of Billy and Kenneth's visit and the fact that they took the medallions. Surothion exploded. "Omnizar sent Billy and Kenneth to steal the medallions, and you guys let them," said Surothion.

"We're very sorry, Surothion. I guess we're not trustworthy enough," said Zomar.

"Sometimes I just want to knock some common sense into your heads," said Surothion.

"We totally blew it, but Kenneth and Billy acted like they were innocent and nothing bad had happened to them," said Cody.

"Never let Omnizar play tricks in your heads. He knows the rules don't have any limit," said Surothion.

Billy and Kenneth returned to Omnizar's dimension. They brought him the medallions, and Omnizar was celebrating that he got away with this one; he was getting ready to release the six witches from the phantom realm.

"Master Omnizar, here are your medallions," said Kenneth.

"Well, thank you, ha-ha. The two of you don't know how much this means to me; I'm so happy for Surothion to lose the seven medallions at the hands of evil," said Omnizar.

"Master Omnizar, I believe it was very silly of Surothion to sleep in his room all morning and let the medallions fall in the wrong hands," said Zervo.

"You have to understand, Zervo. I'm headed to the Minnesota caves. See you later," said Omnizar.

"Wait! Can we come with you just in case of an emergency?" asked Billy.

"Sure. Why not? I don't see a reason for the two of you to not be there," said Omnizar.

Omnizar went to the Minnesota caves with the two Thunder Warriors. When he got there, he began to insert the medallions inside the dark seals that were on the wall. A spell was cast, and the six witches were freed from the phantom destruction and chaos was getting ready to take place.

"This is perfect. I just inserted the medallions inside the dark seals, and a great energy release of power came forth from the infamous phantom realm," said Omnizar.

"We're free after ten million years of imprisonment. I really didn't like that phantom realm since it was destroying our powers," said Zaku.

"You witches can go and destroy the earth. I've released you, and remember that Surothion won't be able to stop any of you. Ha-ha," said Omnizar.

"That name Surothion sounds familiar. He's the legendary leader of those thunder brats. We're going after him, but first we'll destroy the earth. Peace out, Omnizar," said Ination.

After Omnizar released the six dark witches from the phantom realm, they left the Minnesota caves and attacked the city. The dark witches began to capture human souls, and the two Thunder Warriors were helping them destroy the earth. As human souls were being wiped out, the witches saw that their power rapidly increased. The moon had a bloody red color, and so did the earth.

The other Thunder Warriors met at Surothion's lair; they had to do something.

"Surothion, we're in bigger trouble than we thought," said Jennifer.

"Kenneth and Billy are such traitors; they sold us out to Omnizar," said Surothion.

"I know that you are very upset, but we're going to have to bring in the big guns," said Letitia.

"You mean Izon? I'm certain that he will have a huge impact on us defeating those witches," said Surothion.

"Did somebody call my name? Look, I saw Omnizar with Kenneth and Billy. They were celebrating that the witches were free for good," said Izon.

"Here is the plan, Izon. I want you to use your deadliest attack that hasn't been used yet, because this will destroy the grip that the witches have on the moon and sky," said Surothion.

"It is a plan that I see working; I'm going on board with it," said Izon.

"The clock is ticking, and we'd better go. I will attack Kenneth and Billy so I can get them to be on our side," said Surothion.

"You need to watch out for those vampires; maybe they will be there," said Larutio.

"We've got it under control, and everyone should be good to go," said Surothion.

Surothion and the Thunder Warriors, as well as Izon, left Surothion's lair. They went to fight the six witches and the other two Thunder Warriors. This wasn't going to be a fight where they could win that easily.

"So, you guys have come to get wiped out, huh?" said Billy.

"Snap out of it, Billy. This isn't you. You're supposed to be fighting on our side," said Zomar.

"Ay, my head is pounding me. Stop playing with me. The only one who cares about us is Omnizar," said Kenneth.

"Wake up and open your eyes to the truth. Omnizar is just using you. He doesn't treat anyone like they are family," said Randy.

"I can't do this; it's like my mind is fighting for both sides," said Kenneth.

"You're not the only one. I'm feeling the pain too," said Billy.

"It's working. The two of you need to get yourselves together and stop being a hot mess," Supreme Lightning Blaze Surothion shouted.

"Where are we? I don't remember a thing," said Kenneth.

"Thunder Warriors, our powers have doubled, and you can't save the humans," said Ination.

"We shall always united and evil won't stand a chance," zirconium lightning shouted Kenneth.

"Hold on, Thunder Warriors. I'd like to throw in an attack," shouted Ariel Sword Neutron Fury Izon.

"This can't be happening. Ugh, I see that you are destroying the red bloody moon since it is another source of our power," said Zaku.

"Oh, I've picked a direct target. We must hit the medallions on their chest," said Surothion.

"Good job, Izon. You've destroyed the red bloody moon," said Randy.

"Listen closely, Thunder Warriors. If you don't destroy those medallions, then the people will be gone," said Izon.

"You idiots! Do you really think that we will let you destroy our precious medallions? Then this is going to be a fight," Izanero Neton Zaku shouted.

"Remember that the forces of evil don't have any limits. Let's do it," Supreme Lightning Blaze Surothion shouted.

"Ravcon lightning," shouted Jennifer.

"Atomic lightning fury," shouted Cody.

"Neutron lightning," shouted Randy.

"Imperial lightning destroyer," shouted Zomar.

"Ravcon lightning," shouted Letitia.

"Solar lightning destroyer," shouted Jennifer.

"Mystical lightning," shouted Kenneth.

"Yes, we did it! Our attacks successfully destroyed the witches and their medallions," said Billy.

"Know that this is all your fault, Surothion and Izon, because we were this close to destroying the earth," said Ination.

"You witches never had a shot at wiping out the earth. We fought the toughest battle ever," said Surothion.

"Don't blame us for your failures. The power of unity is how we won this battle fair and square. Now, be gone," said Izon.

The attacks that came from Surothion, Izon, and the Thunder Warriors destroyed the six witches and their medallions. This was such a big victory for Surothion and the Thunder Warriors, but Omnizar vowed to seek revenge later on. He decided to take his time before unleashing any demons to launch an assault. The earth was restored to normal, and the Thunder Warriors were the happiest they could be. Izon left and returned to the caves.

Then the Thunder Warriors went to school. But as they were getting ready to put their bags inside their lockers, a fight broke out.

"Dude, I am so exhausted right now. Before we came to school, we should've stopped at the Fusion Burger Shop for a milk shake," said Kenneth.

"I know. I feel like once we're fighting a bad guy, we don't have time to do our daily activities," said Billy.

"That's how it is in life. You make moves that will impact the way you are," said Kenneth.

"I want you to give me whatever money your mother gave to you for lunch," said Lao.

"I don't owe you anything. You're just being a bully. Leave me alone," said Lynx.

"Dude, you just heard her say to leave now," said Randy.

"Listen to me, bud. Stay out of this because it doesn't concern you at all," said Lao.

"Did you just push Lynx to the ground? That does it. I'm taking action," said Randy as he gave Lao a rapid punch.

"Damn, Lao. Randy just knocked you the hell out, dude," said Larutio.

"Hey, what's going on here? I told all of you, no drama during class," said Principal Ben.

"Excuse me, Principal Ben. Lao just pushed me very hard to the ground, and Randy came to help," said Lynx.

"Is that true? As of now I'm suspending Lao for six weeks. Maybe that will be a lesson to him that a man should never put his hands on a woman," said Principal Ben.

"I will tell you the truth, Principal Ben. I was just being a bully by asking her for money," said Lao.

"You should know better. Our school doesn't tolerate troublemakers," said Principal Ben.

"We're headed for class now. You deal with this. Good-bye," said Kenneth.

"I can't keep telling the two of you this. Stop being late for class," said Professor Aaron.

"I'm deeply sorry, Professor Aaron. There was an incident outside in the hallway, and Principal Ben had to step in," said Randy.

"The three of you are excused. Next time just have Principal Ben give you a note," said Professor Aaron.

"I see that everybody has their pen and paper with them," said Larutio.

"That's because the lesson is about foods that can make you sick once you've become a diabetic," said Professor Aaron.

"Speaking of diabetes, type two is the rarest condition since a person can have a relapse and not live," said Jennifer.

"The main thing that bothers me is that having too much sugar can cause a diabetic's blood pressure to explode," said Zomar.

"I am presenting to you guys the pyramid of food; you should be eating all of this healthy stuff," said Professor Aaron.

"You guys are making me so worried. I'm a diabetic too, and taking medication keeps me alive," said Lynx.

"We all need to have cheese, milk, and starch, which are a big part of our diet," said Cody.

"I don't get it. Professor Aaron, if a diabetic needs to eat healthy, then why do they eat fast food and ice cream?" asked Letitia.

"Because they are not seeing the dangers of eating that kind of food; cheeseburgers can cause a clogged artery," said Professor Aaron.

"I try to stay away from fast food since it makes me fifty pounds fatter," said Kenneth.

"I am showing all of you a map that explains the dangers of fast food. If people spend eight years eating fast food, they will have a blood clot inside their brains. All of that fat gets stuck in their blood cells, and this will put them at risk for obesity," said Professor Aaron.

"You've told us a lot. I will continue to live a healthy life," said Angel.

"I'm happy to hear that. Good for you," said Amy.

"Arthritis is another problem that fast food will do to you. Too much fat will make you obese, which can cause your knees to be gone," said Professor Aaron.

"You are what you eat because fast food becomes an addiction that people can't get out of. That addiction will cause your body to be delinquently messed up," said Kenneth.

"The industry doesn't tell you guys the hard cold facts. French fries carry eighty-two grams of oil, and all of that grease is very dangerous," said Arthur.

"I want all of you to write down the steps you will take to make your life better," said Professor Aaron.

"Does it have to involve excising at the gym?" said Zomar.

"It could, but there are hundreds of ways, and I suggest you write them down now," said Professor Aaron.

"All right then; I'm doing it right away," said Zomar.

After class had finished, the Thunder Warriors returned to Surothion's lair.

"I suppose the eight of you had plenty of fun in school, huh?" said Surothion.

"It wasn't that bad to be in class. Besides, the professor is just so creative in every lesson he gives us," said Kenneth.

Surothion got to the point quickly. He said, "The crystals were locked away millions of years ago because there were these three wolves that were vanquished because they terrorized and killed a lot of people. Once the moon turned green, but you have to understand that the moon crystals have been hidden somewhere. If the crystals are found, then chaos is going to take place."

"Whoa. You mean to tell us that werewolves exist and with one swipe of their claws a person can die?" said Billy.

"That's exactly what I'm explaining to you, but you have to remember that the green moon doesn't happen that often. It only occurs once the moon crystals are found," said Surothion.

"Please tell us what you want us to do," said Cody.

"Just go and enjoy your afternoon. If Omnizar sends any of his demons, I will let you know," said Surothion.

"Okay, then, we're leaving, guys. Take Buddy. We will see you in the nighttime," said Larutio.

"I'm asleep during the night, so if you come, just press the alarm. Farewell," said Surothion.

After the Thunder Warriors learned about the moon crystals, they went to Chuck E. Cheese and had some pizza with ice cream. They drank soda, and the eight friends also played Pac-Man and some board games.

"I'm just so glad that we are at Chuck E. Cheese since I haven't been here for a mighty long time," said Zomar.

"You know what? I feel as if we are acting like little children by coming here," said Jennifer.

"I guess that's your opinion, and I can't say too much," said Letitia.

"Here are your large boxes of pizza and a bottle of Pepsi-Cola," said the waitress.

"Thank you very much. The chef did such a great job cooking this pizza," said Randy.

"Our chef is the best one, and he has years of experience in cooking," said the waitress.

"Hmm, the pizza tastes very good, and I love these crusts since they have a lot of cheese on them," said Larutio.

"As a matter of fact, this Pepsi-Cola doesn't have too much sugar like the ones we buy," said Billy.

"Hey, as long as Chuck E. Cheese doesn't disappoint us, I'm good to go," said Cody.

"Sometimes I wonder if life always brings these joyful moments when we get to hang out as friends," said Kenneth.

"Dude, our friendships will last with everybody that's sitting at this table," said Jennifer.

After the Thunder Warriors finished eating pizza and drinking soda at Chuck E. Cheese, they went to a crop farm. They didn't understand that the farm crops had the symbol of the green moon, which wasn't a good sign at all. If the crop symbolizes the green moon, this means that the location of the moon crystals will soon be revealed.

"I've never seen a farm that is this huge in my whole entire life," said Cody.

"Dude, the farm reminds me of the movie *Jeepers Creepers*, the scene where these high school kids get lost inside the bushes," said Zomar.

"All right, since you guys are the first ones here, take a look at the green moon symbols," said Kyle.

"Where did you get them from? You've got no business having the green moon symbols in your possession," said Randy.

"You don't understand. This farm belonged to my grandparents, and they left the farm for me when they passed away," said Kyle.

"Dude, the only reason why we are trying to warn you is that the green moon crystals will be discovered," said Larutio.

"I don't know anything about the moon crystals. My father, who's a great artist, carved the green moon out of these crops," said Kyle.

"We did not know, and I apologize," said Jennifer.

"We're trying to tell you that you must continue to protect the green moon carving because evil is after the moon crystals," said Cody.

"The crops are kept fresh so they can be sold to the farmers' market," said Kyle.

"Kenneth, maybe we should visit a farmers' market and buy some fresh vegetables," said Zomar.

"Dude, it is all right. I can get my fruits and vegetables from the supermarket," said Kenneth.

When the Thunder Warriors visited the crop farm, they weren't allowed to stay because Kyle's father didn't believe them when they tried to tell him about wolves coming to terrorize the people of Minnesota, so they left and went home. Meanwhile, Omnizar was getting ready to summon his next demon; he wanted revenge for the six witches that were destroyed by the Thunder Warriors.

"Ooh, they did it again! This wasn't supposed to happen at all, Zervo. The witches should've succeeded in destroying the Thunder Warriors," said Omnizar.

"Master Omnizar, I guess those witches weren't powerful enough. You could go and hit them hard now," said Zervo.

"You're right. I will make sure that they pay for this dearly. I summon Zagvon to come forth," said Omnizar.

"Master Omnizar, it is an honor to serve," said Zagvon.

"I want you to search for the moon crystals and destroy the Thunder Warriors," said Omnizar.

"It shall be done, and peace out," said Zagvon.

Zagvon went to earth. This deer demon began to unleash transformational solar beams that caused the people to become Armadillatons, giant scorpion demons that would cut the earth open by turning life into dust and destroy everything that existed. Zagvon went to look for the moon crystals inside the Minnesota River. The Thunder Warriors quickly reported to Surothion's lair.

"Omnizar is at it again. He has sent Zagvon, which is his deer demon, to search for the moon crystals by the river," said Surothion.

"I've been hearing a lot of screams outside. The people are seeing these giant scorpion demons that are turning humans into dust; they are destroying the ground by splitting it in two," said Kenneth.

"I see that we have to make a choice. Four Thunder Warriors will come with me, and the other ones will fight the Armadillatons," said Surothion.

"Right. We will see you there later on," said Jennifer.

The Thunder Warriors split up, four of them going with Surothion, and the other four going to fight Zagvon by the Minnesota River.

"Finding these moonstones is so complicated," said Zagvon.

"Hey, don't put your hands into the river," Supreme Lightning Blaze Surothion shouted.

"Ay, you've blasted me on the left shoulder," said Zagvon.

"I'm just doing my job by stopping you from getting those moonstones," said Surothion.

"You've gone too far, you lightning freak, so I'll destroy you now," Zarigonon Fury Zagvon shouted.

"Hold it! We're never far from taking down an enemy," shouted Thunder Striker Kenneth.

"That's right. The Thunder Warriors are here to put evil out of business for good," Thunder Maze Billy shouted.

"Never count me out. This battle is for the chosen ones," Lightning Obliterator Randy shouted.

"Zagvon, you better fall back now," Imperial Lightning Destroyer Zomar shouted.

"You thunder brats, I shall annihilate all of you. I'm very disappointed that my attack didn't have any impact on you," said Zagvon.

"Well, I'm here, and any demon that thinks they will win, then the odds are stacked very much against them," shouted Supreme Lightning Blaze Surothion.

"Don't be an idiot. My force field activates, and it will reflect your attack," said Zagvon.

"Ha-ha. You don't get it then. It's over once my attack strikes you. That is it; you've been destroyed," said Surothion.

"No, I can't believe I've fallen, that I've been defeated," said Zagvon.

"Demons like you should know better than that. Me and my team always have the upper hand. Now, be gone," said Surothion.

"You did such a terrific job, Surothion, in destroying Zagvon," said Randy.

"It takes practice to make perfect. Now, let's get out of here and see how the others are doing," said Surothion.

Surothion and the four Thunder Warriors went to help their friends. They quickly saw that their friends were holding on to the top of the opened ground as the Armadillatons stomped on their hands. This was trouble since Zagvon was destroyed.

"Surothion, help me. We're going to fell into the ditch, and the ground is about to close up," said Larutio.

"Wait a minute. Here, you can take my lightning rope and pass it down to the others quickly," said Surothion.

"Dude, we have to do something about these Armadillatons. They're wreaking havoc upon the earth, upon the wildlife," said Jennifer.

"Since you guys are done getting out of that ditch, form lines and attack all together," said Surothion.

"Say good-bye, Armadillatons," shouted Surenolize Thunder Jennifer.

"Astro lightning," shouted Randy.

"Proton lightning fury," shouted Zomar.

"Mercury lightning," shouted Cody.

"And now I will add the finishing touches," shouted Supreme Lightning Blaze Surothion.

The attacks that came from Surothion and the Thunder Warriors destroyed the Armadillatons, and the wildlife was restored. "I was very disappointed that we didn't come close to finding those moonstones," said Letitia.

"Oh, just stop it. It's not like the moonstones are going to fall out of the sky," said Cody.

"Guys, we'd better get back. We were watching a bank robbery take place at Chase Bank," said Kenneth.

"I want everyone to get on the ground and put their hands on the backs of their heads," said the robber.

"Hey, I suggest you drop your weapon now," said Larutio.

"A punk like you don't have any business interfering in this, so say good-bye," said the robber.

"Your bullets are no match for me," shouted Proton Lightning Fury Larutio.

"Please, I beg you, stop electrocuting me before I die," said the robber.

"You won't die; you'll just feel some pain in your body," said Larutio.

"There might be two other robbers inside the bank. I'm calling the cops now," said Billy.

"I knew that this was a bad idea," said the robber.

"Your friends shouldn't of put you up to this. Did you guys really think that you would walk away with a bag of money? It doesn't work like that," said Larutio.

"Is this the robber we've been looking for?" asked Officer Brand.

"Yes, it is. He's been committing a string of robberies, and the day he's been caught has arrived," said Kenneth.

"This loser is going away for a long time, along with his buddies," said Officer Brand.

"Just give me a minute so I can explain myself. The only reason why I committed this crime was because I didn't have any money to pay my family members back," said the robber.

The police were happy that the Thunder Warriors were able to stop the robbery before a life was taken, and thankfully no one had gotten hurt.

So then the eight friends headed to the ice cream factory so they could get a little heads-up on how ice cream was made.

"Hi. Welcome to the ice cream shop. Today we are going to show you how everything is made ice cream style," said Sandy.

"Wow, the ice cream shop is pretty interesting and cool," said Zomar.

"Over here the workers take the cream of milk, and they put it inside a freezer for half an hour. Once it's frozen, then we will have our vanilla ice cream that we want," said Sandy.

"It must take you guys a whole month to sell and ship these ice cream bars," said Cody.

"Our business is in demand, and we pay our workers twenty-five bucks per hour," said Sandy.

"At least that's a decent wage and not cheap labor," said Jennifer.

"Sandy, I wish we could stay longer, but hey, me and my friends have some personal things to do," said Letitia.

"It's all right. I'm not stopping any of you from leaving; go ahead," said Sandy.

After the Thunder Warriors visited the ice cream shop, they returned to Surothion's lair.

He greeted them by saying, "I've got some exciting news for everyone. I have found the moonstones."

"That's great. How did you do it?" asked Zomar.

"Izon found the moonstones on Mars; they came to him in a vision," said Surothion.

"What do we have to do now so Omnizar doesn't find out?" asked Kenneth.

"All of you are going to Mars with Izon. So am I. We're teleporting there right now," said Surothion.

"At last the moonstones shall be mine, and Master Omnizar shall have his way," said Zervo.

"Maybe you'd better go back to where you came from, Zervo, because I'm not handing the stones to nobody," said Izon.

"You and the Thunder Warriors won't leave Mars; I will destroy all of you," said Zervo.

"I'm warning you. Don't come any closer. That is it," shouted Ariel Sword Neutron Fury Izon.

"You heard him. You're putting yourself in big danger by not listening," shouted Supreme Lightning Blaze Surothion.

"This is unbelievable. You blasted me with your sword, and Surothion's attack has wounded me," said Zervo.

"Zervo, we knew that Omnizar was going to try and make it to Planet Mars before we did, and that is why Izon bailed us out on this one," said Larutio.

"You puny Thunder Warriors will pay for this. Until next time we meet again, farewell, thunder bums," said Zervo.

"Go ahead and run like the coward you are. Tell Omnizar the Thunder Warriors are alive and well," said Cody.

"You guys, we've done it. Our work is finished for now. We're out of here," said Surothion.

After the Thunder Warriors, Surothion, and Izon were able to get the moonstones, they left Planet Mars and returned to Surothion's lair. Surothion discussed a safe location to keep the moonstones in.

"I will be keeping the moonstones inside my coat pocket," said Surothion.

"Your coat pocket isn't a safe place since a vampire would throw you to the ground and steal them," said Randy.

"Come on. Stop talking nonsense. Nobody is going to touch me. Besides, I would do a much better job than you guys would," said Surothion.

"Since you're the leader, you do whatever works best," said Billy.

"Dude, let's not talk about these moonstones anymore," said Cody.

"Take care, Surothion, and have a good afternoon," said Zomar.

"Believe me, I will try to enjoy the day by refreshing my mind," said Surothion.

The Thunder Warriors left Surothion's lair. They were driving their car home, but trouble was getting ready to take place. A group of bikers surrounded their car and began to follow them around. But the bikers were surprised when fireballs began falling from the sun and the bikers were getting burned. The Thunder Warriors didn't understand that the fireballs were being caused by the atomic star from outer space; this meant trouble for them because anyone who was walking in the streets or driving their car would get burned by the fireballs coming from the sun.

"Every time we go on these adventures, it feels like we're gone for at least a couple days," said Billy.

"You know how Surothion will be most of the time, and that's how the mission has been," said Jennifer.

"We have again found ourselves in an unsafe situation; a group of bikers is following us," said Randy.

"Kenneth, put your foot on top of that pedal and drive now," said Larutio.

"Dude, I'm doing that just now. We're taking off—yahoo," said Kenneth.

"Hang on a minute, dude Look out for those fireballs that are coming from the sky; you wouldn't want your car to catch on fire," said Cody.

"Wow, I'm stunned. The fireballs drove the bikers away from your car, and they're riding their motorcycles away very fast," said Letitia.

"I seriously can't look because the fireballs are causing chaos in the city; it could be the heat wave that's doing this damage," said Billy.

"Maybe we should stop at your house due to an emergency," said Larutio.

"You guys can come to my place until you're able to get home," said Kenneth.

The Thunder Warriors went to Kenneth's house so they could be safe and try to figure out the cause of these fireballs coming from the sun, but they didn't have any luck until they began to use their telescope.

"Is it me, or is the sun hotter than an oven?" asked Cody.

"The sun's heat wave is reaching its maximum level, and we can't do too much about it," said Randy.

"If we set foot outside, then the grass is going to catch on fire before we even know it," said Zomar.

"Kenneth, you need to use your telescope and check out the stars," said Billy.

"I've got the telescope right here. Just give me some space so I can take a closer look," said Kenneth.

"Hang on a second. I'm seeing these solar waves coming from the air. We might be in some serious trouble sooner than we thought," said Letitia.

"Guys, the atomic star is shooting beams into the sun; that is why the heat wave is increasing and these fireballs are hitting the earth," said Kenneth.

"We've never heard of this atomic star. Maybe it's a bomb designed to destroy Planet Earth," said Billy.

"There has to be ways to contain the atomic star before we're doomed," said Cody.

"I've got a suggestion. Maybe Surothion knows the way to stop this atomic star," said Jennifer.

"Let's go to his lair now before the earth is annihilated," said Randy.

The Thunder Warriors quickly went to Surothion's lair; they wanted to find a way to stop the destruction that was taking place.

"Surothion, you have to urgently help us out with this one," said Kenneth.

"I know the damage that is being caused by the atomic star, and we need to take affirmative action," said Surothion.

"I've figured out something: you should use the powers of the moonstones to stop this atomic star," said Cody.

"That sounds like a great idea, but I tell you, we're going into outer space now," said Surothion.

Surothion took the Thunder Warriors into space. He was going to use the moonstones on the atomic star. He knew that anything deadly that was used on the moonstones would bring forth the three werewolves within twenty-two weeks, but even though this was a deadly risk, he went with it anyway.

"I don't want any of you to get too close to the atomic star because it will shoot a blast beam at you," said Surothion.

"We will just let you handle the situation in a safe manner," said Zomar.

"All right then; watch and learn," shouted Supreme Lightning Blaze Surothion.

"I see that the atomic star isn't shooting any more beams into the sun," said Larutio.

"Every one of us can go home now," said Jennifer.

"Surothion, you saved the day, buddy. We're just so grateful to have you on our side," said Letitia.

"Letitia, when the going gets tough, I intend to stand taller and defeat the problem," said Surothion.

"It certainly feels a lot cooler and even chilly while being in space," said Letitia.

After Surothion finished stopping the atomic star from shooting more energy beams into the sun, he returned to his lair. The Thunder Warriors went to school.

"I really like it when you guys come to class before the bell rings," said Professor Aaron.

"We wouldn't want any tardiness on our report card because this might lead to a bad report to an employer," said Zomar.

"It's good to hear that from you. Today's lesson is about being attacked by a gang," said Professor Aaron.

"If I were to ever be attacked by a gang, it wouldn't look good for me at all; I would be forced to defend myself," said Cody.

"But, Professor Aaron, these gangs are everywhere, committing illegal activities," said Billy.

"Now I'm jumping into the dark part of the lesson: trying to defend yourself doesn't always work once the situation becomes hostile," said Professor Aaron.

"I always carry a Taser in my purse because you don't know if the perpetrator would ever try to take your life," said Jennifer.

"That's why we've got officers on every street corner—to keep you safe," said Professor Aaron.

"We know that the gangs are causing chaos, but come on, you don't see them that often around Minnesota," said Letitia.

"You're right, and trouble isn't something that we would ever seek in our lives," said Larutio.

"Flip your books to page 115. What you're seeing is the police surrounding a house. It involves an individual with a gun, but this is only fiction and emergency training," said Professor Aaron.

"I'm seeing dramatic moments of hostages being rescued," said Kenneth.

"Lynx, I would like for you to read for us," said Professor Aaron.

"When the gang era began in the 1980s, police had to go to the streets of California and make a clean sweep by putting violent gang members into prison. Today young men try to join gangs because they want to fit in and be cool," said Lynx.

"Thanks for reading for us. Everybody may close their books since the lesson has ended. When you get home, think about this lesson. You never know; one day one of you may find yourselves in that particular situation. Good-bye and peace out," said Professor Aaron.

After the lesson had ended, the eight Thunder Warriors went to play volleyball. Meanwhile, Omnizar was getting ready to summon his next demon.

"Zervo, how could you let Izon defeat you on Planet Mars with Surothion?" asked Omnizar.

"Master Omnizar, it wasn't my fault; I was outnumbered. Izon attacked with his sword, and I was badly wounded," said Zervo.

"It's okay. I promise you that the Thunder Warriors won't destroy this demon. I summon Razio to come forth," said Omnizar.

"Master Omnizar, as you can clearly see, the Thunder Warriors would have to follow me inside the dream realm, which they won't, so I will obliterate those humans. Ha-ha," said Razio.

"That sounds excellent. Go now," said Omnizar.

"Farewell, Master Omnizar, and you take care," said Razio.

Razio went to earth. Once he got there, he began to get inside people's dreams. His first target was Lynx; this nightmare that she was having was going to be very terrorizing and harmful.

"Mom, I can't believe that you are here with me. I thought that you passed away," said Lynx.

"Honey, I'm not dead; it is just fiction. I'm still living inside my spirit," said Miss Orkney.

"I missed you dearly when I saw your body lying inside the casket," said Lynx.

A moment later, Lynx was trying to escape from the dream. "No, this isn't real. Your face is peeling off. Let go of me," said Lynx.

"Ha-ha, I refuse to let go of your hand, young girl. You shall remain inside the dream dimension as your human soul fades away. Farewell," said Razio.

"No, I can't be dying. I've always lived a decent life," said Lynx.

"Since you were my first victim, it won't hurt me to cry at all good-byes," said Razio.

After Razio imprisoned Lynx within her dream, she began to die slowly. Razio was moving on to his next victim, which was Mr. Harris, the assistant administrator at Star Field University. Mr. Harris saw zombies chasing him, but as he was being chased, a stranger grabbed his hand and he started turning to snake oil.

"Hello, Mr. Harris. We've come to destroy you," said the zombie.

"No, I can't be trapped in Zombieland. I'm just dreaming," said Mr. Harris.

"Mr. Harris, I can help, but you have to agree to give up your human soul," said Zotu.

"I'm not trading my life for some sick twisted dimension that involves me," said Mr. Harris.

"Well then, since you were just being very dumbfounded, you shall suffer the consequences," said Razio.

"I can't feel my hand because it is turning to snake oil," said Mr. Harris.

"Since you were my second victim, I have to leave you alone. Now, peace out," said Razio.

"Please show mercy for me. I'm innocent. I didn't do anything wrong," said Mr. Harris.

"Well, that's too bad. You'll never live again or see the life you once had."

Razio terrorized two victims and then moved on to his third victim, Miss Terry. She found herself unable to get away from what was about to take place in her dream, which was very disturbing.

"Harold, I thought you were dead and we buried you," said Terry.

"Honey, sweetheart, I'm not dead. You're just living a fantasy inside your mind," said Harold.

"This sounds too good to be true. Are you sure that you're real?"

"Of course I am, honey. Just go to sleep," said Harold.

"Your face is melting, and I see venom stingers all around your body," said Terry.

"I told you that my spirit was alive and I didn't die; it's just that this isn't me at all," said Harold.

"Oh no, someone, help me; my life is over," yelled Terry.

"Miss Terry, everything went well; you were the perfect victim," said Razio.

"You vicious demon, I guarantee you that somebody will find you and shred you to pieces and destroy you," said Miss Terry.

"I doubt that will ever happen since your destruction is taking place right now," said Razio.

"Ay, my body is turning into mud. Yuk," said Miss Terry.

"I suppose this is good-bye for you, Miss Terry," said Razio.

"Somebody, please send help for me," said Miss Terry.

Razio then moved on to the next victim, but Surothion had found out that all of this was happening. He brought the Thunder Warriors together, and they were going to come up with a plan to destroy Razio, but this was going to be very difficult since they had to find a way to get to the dream realm.

"Surothion, we've found ourselves in big trouble, and you have to be there for us," said Kenneth.

"I know what you mean, Kenneth. Omnizar has summoned his demon Razio, and this demon is terrorizing people in their sleep. I want all of you to take a look at the screen. These three people have been Razio's victims," said Surothion.

"Unbelievable. That's Lynx and Mr. Harris, as well as Miss Terry," said Billy.

"The problem that we've got is that these three people have died in their sleep because Razio has killed them," said Surothion.

"Hold on. I don't even think that we could find Razio since he is inside the dream realm. How do we get there?" asked Randy.

"I absolutely agree with Randy. We've never been inside the dream realm before," said Cody.

"I get what both of you are saying, but I've figured out a way the moonstones will open the gate for us. Watch and learn," said Surothion.

"Wow, that's very awesome. The gate to the dream realm is very huge," said Larutio.

"All right. Here are the plans. We're going to find Razio once we get inside the dream realm and destroy it," said Surothion.

"You are such an intelligent ally because you know the tricks and trades of how to stop evil," said Zomar.

"I'm your leader. I always think ahead and brilliantly," said Surothion.

Surothion and the Thunder Warriors went inside the dream realm so they could stop Razio, but as they arrived there, they caught Razio getting ready to target his next victim. The nine of them stood behind the bushes and waited for when it was time to attack Razio.

"I find this to be very strange. I'm inside the forest, and it looks too scary," said Carol.

"Carol, I love that dress you are wearing," said Danny.

"Huh? Danny, that's crazy. You died in a car accident fourteen years ago," said Carol.

"But, sweetheart, you know me. All I care about is loving you and treating you with respect," said Danny.

"You better get away from her now, Razio," said Surothion.

"What's he talking about? I thought that this was you," said Carol.

"Don't listen to him. He's lying to you. This is me, and I'm dead ass," said Danny.

"Listen to me, Carol. This isn't your man. It's a demon trying to kill you," said Surothion.

"I absolutely believe him since your face is turning into dust," said Carol.

"Look, Surothion, you'd better not get any closer, or I will inject this stinger inside her neck," said Razio.

"Carol, move aside quickly now," Supreme Lightning Blaze Surothion shouted.

"You've destroyed nearly half of me—ay," said Razio.

"That's what you get for causing terror," said Surothion.

"It's a good thing I jumped away fast, or I would've been struck by lightning," said Carol.

"Even if I'm destroyed, you won't be able to save the last three victims since the sand of time is ticking and they are almost gone," Rizko Zacon Razio shouted.

"We will indeed be able to save them," Surenolize Thunder Jennifer shouted.

"Wait, let me add to the devastating assault," Ariel Sword Neutron Fury Izon shouted.

"Proton lightning," shouted Randy.

"Razio, we guarantee you that your fate is done and over with," Thunder Striker Kenneth shouted.

"And now I shall pitch in the finishing touches," Lamecnia's Thunder Larutio shouted.

The attacks that came from Surothion, Izon, and the Thunder Warriors destroyed Razio. Surothion had come up with a plan to save the three victims, so the group revisited their dreams.

"I feel very terrible for Lynx; she's a young girl who doesn't deserve any of this," said Letitia.

"Guys, I know that your feelings are deeply hurt, and I will restore the loved ones. We've lost the moonstones. Activate energy reformation," said Surothion.

"Lynx is waking up from her nightmare. So are Mr. Harris and Miss Terry," said Cody.

"I told you that I would bring them back, and now they can live peaceful lives," said Surothion.

"Our work is done for the day. Let's go," said Izon.

After Surothion had restored the people back to their lives, the group left the dream realm and returned home. Billy invited his friends to his house.

"Billy, I see that you invited your buddies over," said Miss Carney.

"Mom, you know how my friends are. They just want to hang out after a long day of work," said Billy.

"I'm not saying I don't want them to come over here, but my house is a mess and dinner isn't ready yet," said Miss Carney.

"I should've waited until it was five o'clock to let them come here. I apologize, Mom," said Billy.

"You can just go and sit in the living room with them so I can prepare the dinner," said Miss Carney.

"We will do just that. Hey, I just saw the moon turn green. Something is going on here," said Randy.

"Thunder Warriors, can you read me? Come in," said Surothion.

"Our lightning bracelets have activated, and it's Surothion," said Larutio.

"We can hear you, Surothion," said Zomar.

"I need all of you to report to my lair now due to an emergency," said Surothion.

"We're coming now; just give us a few minutes," said Cody.

"All right then. I'll see you once you get here. Farewell," said Surothion.

After the Thunder Warriors were contacted by Surothion, they went to his lair because the green moon continued to grow and the three werewolves were getting ready to terrorize the people.

"I see that all of you got my message and you came," said Surothion.

"We saw the green moon approaching, and that is why we're going to have to react now," said Jennifer.

"I'm very concerned about the green moon. It will release these blast beams that will destroy you guys," said Surothion.

"We will try to be very careful and avoid getting hit by these blast beams; the blast beams shouldn't be a problem at all," said Billy.

"I have to warn you guys about these werewolves. They are not your average wolves that will jump from building to building. They shoot firebombs out of their mouths to destroy their prey, and they fly in the air; their wings are as sharp as knives," said Surothion.

"Whoa. Thanks for telling us. I'm very worried now. Once these werewolves get a taste of our fury, they should be destroyed," said Letitia.

"I believe we're leaving now; we can't let chaos reign," said Zomar.

The Thunder Warriors went with Surothion so they could fight the werewolves. Izon came to help also.

"You Thunder Warriors are punks because your useless attacks won't work," said Wolfisatro.

"That's what you think. Guess again," Thunder Striker Kenneth shouted.

"Hold it right there. Since my powers make me immune to lightning attacks, this should be a knockout punch," Astro Firebombs Wolfisatro shouted.

"Ay, you guys have to help me. These firebombs are burning me," said Kenneth.

"You should've moved to the curb quickly. I've got this," Supreme Lightning Blaze Surothion shouted.

"No, this can't be possible. Your attack destroyed my defense wings that shielded me," said Wolfisatro.

"Oh, I thought that you said you were immune to lightning. Get your mind out of the gutter," said Surothion.

"Surothion, you caused us to become very upset. Since Wolfisatro's wings are destroyed, you'll pay for that," Mystical Flair Wolfinatar shouted.

"This one is mine; I won't let these werewolves cause any more damage," Ariel Sword Neutron Fury Izon shouted.

"Help me. The attack that came from Izon has vanquished me," said Wolfinatar.

"Since I'm the only one left, Surothion, you won't dodge this one," Azon Fury Wolferaso shouted.

"Who said anything about me dodging an attack? I intend to stand and fight," Supreme Lightning Blaze Surothion shouted.

"Ravcon lightning," shouted Jennifer.

"Proton lightning," shouted Randy.

"Mercury lightning," shouted Cody.

The attacks that came from Surothion, Izon, and the Thunder Warriors destroyed the three werewolves. Surothion saw something he had never seen before: the moonstones disappeared after the werewolves were destroyed, and the green moon disappeared as well. The earth was restored back to normal, and then the Thunder Warriors went back to school.

"Today's lesson is about beating the odds and overcoming failure in life," said Professor Aaron.

"I've had a lot of failures in my lifetime, but the lesson I learned was you must not let setbacks make you feel discouraged," said Lynx.

"Sometimes we'll all fall down, and we have to work our way to get back up from the ground," said Jennifer.

"I am writing on the board. The number one thing we all face in life are obstacles and criticism," said Professor Aaron.

"I always try to not let any of the criticism get to me by just focusing on the positive, not the negative," said Larutio.

"To me failure means that we must put in more effort in order to achieve our goals in life," said Letitia.

"Every day people try to do the right thing, but they get caught up in negativity crap that will impact their emotional thinking," said Billy.

"There are two things a person must do: you have a cause and an effect," said Davis.

"We must all try to become team leaders because a leader of the group knows what he's doing and he doesn't pay any attention to those who aren't up to his level yet," said Professor Aaron.

"I think that a person who is smart shouldn't waste his or her time on someone who's doing nothing with their life," said Morel.

"All right now, I'm switching over to the other part of the lesson—how does negative mind-set affect people? I see that Angeline has raised her hand," said Professor Aaron.

"A negative mind-set can lead to someone committing crimes," said Angeline.

"That is correct. Speaking of committing crimes, a lot of eighteen-year-olds listen to their friends; that may cause them to go to prison," said Professor Aaron.

"Professor Aaron, I object to this lesson because it questions people's state of mental health," said Jennifer.

"I know how you feel, Jennifer, but when people bully others, this can lead them to make a decision that won't really hurt them," said Professor Aaron.

"I like to smile and not be angry with others," said Kenneth.

"You see, this is exactly what I was talking about; having a smooth attitude is nice," said Randy.

"You guys haven't quite fully understood the meaning of success. It will come to you once that college degree is in your hand," said Professor Aaron.

"Hold on a minute. I've got a lot of research to do, and I'm just asking everybody not to compare me to the in-crowd," said Cody.

"I've got plenty of assignments for you guys. When you get home today, I want you to go to the library and use the computer for your homework. Take one of the sheets and pass around the rest," said Professor Timothy.

"You have to believe me, I am going to spend a lot of time working on this assignment," said Peterson.

"You are allowed to spend as much time as you want; nobody is stopping you. Class has ended, and everybody can go home," said Professor Aaron.

After class was over the Thunder Warriors did something that they weren't supposed to do: they went drag racing with two other members of their class.

"So, Lynx, are you scared to drag race us or what?" asked Jennifer.

"I'm not afraid to do anything that involves racing, so let's go now," said Lynx.

"Look, Larutio, it will be us versus her and Brandon," said Letitia.

"Hey now, you wait a minute. We've got a lot of fight in us, and I've never lost a drag race in my whole life," said Brandon.

"Let's go and see how you match up against me. Raise the white flag, Larutio," said Jennifer.

"Are you guys ready? On the count of one, two, three, on your mark, get set, go," said Larutio.

"Ha-ha, Lynx, I thought that you were a very fast driver. What happened to you?" asked Kenneth.

"You're not being fair at all by cutting me off and jumping in front of my car," said Lynx.

"That's how the race has been. The fastest driver speeds in front of the one behind me. See you later," said Billy.

"I will catch up to you; just trust me," said Lynx.

"Jennifer, you can't even drive faster than me, you slowpoke," said Brandon.

"I'll show you who's slow. Just look at my car. Now you see me; now you don't. Farewell," said Jennifer.

"Cheater! You bump rushed my car so you could move ahead," said Brandon.

"I demand that all of you stop your cars now. Undercover police," said the officer.

"I can't believe that we got busted. That is so sad," said Billy.

"You college punks know that we don't tolerate drag racing in the streets of Star Field," said Officer Linksu.

"Officer, it was just a misunderstanding. Me and my friends were just partying the night," said Cody.

"Today just isn't my day. I arrested one hundred drug traffickers and eighty-five drunk drivers," said Officer Maxine.

"We deeply apologize for the trouble that was caused," said Letitia.

"Say it to the judge when he sets your bail," said Officer Kenny.

"We will be keeping our mouths shut since it will make you angry," said Zomar.

After the police officers took the eight friends to the police station, their mug shots were taken. Lynx and Brandon were able to get away. The eight friends weren't very happy about the prison term. They were brought before a court judge, and he set their bail for one thousand dollars.

"Hello, college brats. I see that you got yourselves in some trouble," said Judge John.

"Your Honor, I ask that you show mercy for us and not put us in prison for a long time," said Kenneth.

"I am going to set your bail at one thousand dollars each. If the bail money is paid tonight, then all of you can go home," said Judge John.

"You are such a nice judge. I promise that next time we won't come back to this courtroom," said Zomar.

"Guards, take them back to their holding cells until a relative comes," said Judge John.

"All right, Your Honor, it shall be done," said Officer Kenny.

"Guys, you don't know how excited I am that the judge didn't impose a very harsh penalty on us and we didn't get any fines," said Billy.

"We deserved it. It's not like the rest of us had cds substances on us," said Randy.

"You guys have a visitor. He paid your bails, and all of you are free to go," said Officer Linkso.

"I am so glad to hear this news. Freedom feels good," said Larutio.

"Whoever paid our bails, may God bless him," said Jennifer.

"Good luck to all of you, and stay out of trouble for good," said Officer Maxine.

After Surothion finished paying the bail money for each and every Thunder Warrior to be free, they returned to his lair. But Omnizar was up to no good again; he was getting ready to summon his next demon.

"Zervo, this just pisses me off. Those damn Thunder Warriors defeated the three werewolves and the green moon," said Omnizar.

"Master Omnizar, it really doesn't matter that those werewolves were destroyed. You can always gain the upper hand," said Zervo.

"You know what? Surothion won't get away this time. I summon Arckleton to come forth," said Omnizar.

"Look, Master Omnizar, I'm going to obliterate those Thunder Warriors. Farewell," said Arckleton.

Arckleton went to earth. Once he arrived there, he was turning the people into mud pits. The people of Star Field City saw these slippery mudslides, and the Thunder Warriors and Surothion were trying to figure out how they could find Arckleton.

"Okay, Thunder Warriors, the situation that we're in is very slippery," said Surothion.

"Omnizar has summoned a mud demon that's causing these mudslides that are wiping everything out," said Kenneth.

"I certainly don't want my clothes to get caught up in those mud pits; they sound very nasty," said Billy.

"We can't find the mud demon since it is quickly scattering all over the place," said Randy.

"Maybe Izon could help us get rid of these mud pits," said Larutio.

"I am going to try to insert my sword into the ground. Maybe that will slow down Arckleton," said Izon.

The Thunder Warriors, Izon, and Surothion went to fight Arckleton. They knew that the mud pit would be hovering all over their clothes, but they weren't worried at all.

"Surothion, I should be the first one to make a move," Ariel Sword Neutron Fury Izon shouted.

"Let's amp it up now," Supreme Lightning Blaze Surothion shouted.

"Ravcon lightning," shouted Jennifer.

"Zirconium lightning," shouted Kenneth.

"Proton lightning fury," shouted Billy.

"Mercury lightning," shouted Cody.

"Tirol lightning," shouted Larutio.

"Fusion lightning fury," shouted Randy.

"Astro lightning," shouted Randy.

"All right; it's working. The mud pit is starting to fade, and Arckleton is being exposed," said Letitia.

"No, this wasn't supposed to happen. The humans were almost destroyed, but now that's never going to happen since you've interrupted me," said Arckleton.

"Your reign of terror ends now," Ariel Sword Neutron Fury Izon shouted.

"Izon, your attack will only tickle me; ha-ha," Arcklerato Neutron Arckleton shouted.

"Wait, I'll back you up, Izon," Supreme Lightning Blaze Surothion shouted.

The attacks that came from Surothion, Izon, and the Thunder Warriors destroyed Arckleton, and the earth was restored to normal. Then the Thunder Warriors learned from Surothion about the dragon winger symbols; whoever possesses these symbols will cause these beasts to awaken and destroy the earth with their deadly fire.

"I'm trying to tell you, guys, that we got away with destroying the last demon, but this time nothing will be easy for us," said Surothion.

"Are you saying there is somebody that is more powerful than us?" asked Kenneth.

"There are these four beasts known as dragon wingers. They have sixteen dragon wings, but there is a key problem: they use their fire flames to destroy the earth," said Surothion.

"So you are telling us there are dragons among us," said Cody.

"No, these dragon beasts are for real. Their fire can destroy the whole entire planet, but you have to remember these beasts were defeated by the sacred imprisonment symbol," said Surothion.

"Whoa, that sounds very incredible. I wonder how we stop them from being released," said Kenneth.

"We can't stop them since they are imprisoned within the dragon symbols. You guys must not let four people come together. If they do, then the dragon symbols will be activated," said Surothion.

"Come on; you are telling us too much. We're going home, guys," said Jennifer.

"You have to have patience. Surothion just gave us some cold facts about the next mission," said Zomar.

"I guess he was just in a rush to conclude," said Letitia.

"I'm feeling kind of sleepy. We definitely have to go home before I fall on this floor and sleep," said Randy.

After Surothion told the Thunder Warriors about the dragon wingers, they went home. Meanwhile the four friends that possessed the dragon winger symbols were in the forest camping.

"The forest is just like us being at the park playing football," said Julia.

"I find that there is nothing creepy about the forest besides us all having fun and relaxing," said Duke.

"The two of you are such moochers, I can tell that you both are in love," said Samberg.

"They aren't in love. I was just sitting down beside them having a good time," said Sarah.

"Whoa, this shouldn't be happening here. My dragon symbol is glowing very brightly," said Duke.

"Mine too. But my mom told me that we were meant to have these symbols since the day we were born," said Julia.

"No, I'm very hot, and I feel my body is getting ready to explode," said Samberg.

"Don't worry. You're not going to die. I feel the dragons are being released from the symbols," said Sara.

"I suggest that we get out of here now. The dragon wingers are here," said Duke.

"I'm with you on this; we're out of here now," said Julia.

After the four friends came together and the four dragon beasts were set free, they left the force because they decided that it was best for them to go home and not get burned by the fire that was coming from the four dragons.

"Larutio, you better jump to the curb quickly before that fire cooks you alive," said Jennifer.

"I'm jumping right now; that was a close one," said Larutio.

"I don't even think that we should get any closer to the fire since it's extremely hot," said Surothion.

"Surothion, the four dragon beasts are causing too much chaos; we must react now," said Izon.

"I'm trying very hard. We can't make an attack since the dragon wingers are firing their flames too quickly," said Surothion.

"I refuse to sit by and like all of you not do something," Thunder Striker Kenneth shouted.

"Kenneth, it's too dangerous for you. I'm afraid you'll get killed by those dragon wingers," said Letitia.

"Thunder Warriors, stand down. Me and Surothion got this battle," Ariel Sword Neutron Fury Izon shouted.

"All right, old friend; it's just like last time," Supreme Lightning Blaze Surothion shouted.

"I won't stand down. The day we were born as Thunder Warriors, we made a promise to the people of this city. Ravcon lightning," shouted Jennifer.

"Proton lightning fury," shouted Billy.

"Mercury lightning," shouted Randy.

"Astro lightning," shouted Zomar.

"Fusion lightning," shouted Letitia.

The attacks that came from Surothion, Izon, and the Thunder Warriors were so devastating that they completely destroyed the dragon wingers. This stopped the destruction that was taking place. Then they all went home.

Then the Thunder Warriors did something that they weren't supposed to do: they broke into a newsroom so they could get information about the alpha vampires, a group of vampires that couldn't be killed or destroyed.

"Kenneth, you go to the drawer inside the office. We need to get this alpha vampire information for Surothion," said Jennifer.

"Don't speak very loud because you never know. They might have you on some kind of tape recorder, so speak in a low tone," said Billy.

"Guys, watch out for the cameras; they could be watching us," said Larutio.

"Cody, how could you? I didn't say for you to blast that camera. What if you were seen?" said Zomar.

"I'm trying to be careful. I see that Jennifer has found a suitcase from the left drawer," said Randy.

"Okay, guys, we're going to sneak out slowly. I suggest that none of you try to trigger the alarm. Just walk slowly outside," said Jennifer.

"Ooh, you triggered the alarm, and the police are on their way," said Letitia.

"It's not my fault. I didn't mean to do it. We'd better come up with another way to make our exit," said Randy.

"Thunder Warriors, I'm getting all of you out of here now since there are 150 cop cars outside. Let's go," said Surothion.

Surothion took the Thunder Warriors from the newsroom to his lair. They were going to reveal to him what they found, but the alpha vampires were in town causing chaos.

"You guys were lucky that prison wasn't knocking at your door," said Surothion.

"We were just trying to get the information for you by being there," said Kenneth.

"You guys don't get it. As your leader I'm trying to keep a closer eye on all of you," said Surothion.

"I understand what you're saying, but we want to make sure that the mission is complete," said Zomar.

"I'm picking up a lot of chaos in Star Field City. The alpha vampires are back, and we must go before they strike at least one hundred people," said Surothion.

"Wait! Before we go out, you should take a look at the suitcase. It has some important papers inside of it," said Jennifer.

"I'm very shocked at what I'm seeing. The alpha vampires are created from indestructible vaccines," said Surothion.

"We have to find those vaccine plants and destroy them," said Randy.

"We'll talk more about that later," said Surothion.

Surothion and the Thunder Warriors went to fight the alpha vampires.

"You Thunder Warriors need to leave town now," said Lasso.

"We're not going anywhere. It's you who should be running for your lives," said Surothion.

"You dare to defy us. You must not have heard that Star Field City belongs to us," said Racknis.

"Stop talking nonsense. This city isn't yours. Besides, the people are just trying to enjoy their lives," Supreme Lightning Blaze Surothion shouted.

"Your attack has diminished our vaccine, and you'll pay for that," Quaralizer Lasso shouted.

"All right, guys. Surothion did his part; now it's our turn. Ravcon lightning," shouted Jennifer.

"Zirconium lightning," shouted Kenneth.

"Proton lightning fury," shouted Randy.

"Mercury lightning," shouted Zomar.

"Astro lightning," shouted Larutio.

"Ezorion lightning," shouted Cody.

"I see that your attacks are now damaging the alpha pack, so I'll handle the rest," Ariel Sword Neutron Fury Izon shouted.

The attacks that came from Izon, Surothion, and the Thunder Warriors destroyed the alpha pack's indestructible vaccine that was giving them superpowers, and the three of them were back to normal. The Thunder Warriors left and went home, and so did Surothion. But Omnizar was getting ready to summon his next demon; he was furious that Surothion had taken down his alpha pack.

"Surothion has too much nerve inside him. Curse those thunder losers for destroying my alpha pack. I heard that they will be looking for the plants that contain those vaccines, but let's see how they fight the cold. I summon Ravacu to come forth," said Omnizar.

"Master Omnizar, oh, I say thunder can't stop ice since water conducts electricity," said Zervo.

"I won't fail you, Master Omnizar. I'm very certain that those Thunder Warriors will become ice picks. Ha-ha," said Ravacu.

Ravacu went to earth. When he arrived there, he began to turn the earth into an ice field. The Thunder Warriors knew that being cold could make them sick, but they weren't concerned because their powers protected them from the cold. Ravacu continued to use his deadly ice to obliterate the planet. He could not be found anywhere. The Thunder Warriors were trying to make it to school, but this was not going to be a simple operation.

"Are you guys cold, or is it just me that's feeling the chilly breeze?" asked Kenneth.

"I'm not cold. It's just the snow that's falling from the sky," said Cody.

"Well, I doubt that we will be able to make it to the university since there is an ice mountain hovering all over it," said Larutio.

"Man, screw these damn ice storms; it's just not fair at all," said Billy.

"I think that we're trapped and there is no way out for us," said Jennifer.

"All of you should be paying close attention because I see a homeless man sitting on the sidewalk," said Letitia.

"We would not want him to freeze to death, so you guys better give him your blanket," said Zomar.

"Sure. I'll be happy to do that since I really deeply truly care," said Randy.

"Sir, here you go. You can have this nice large fluffy blanket and a couple of hundred dollars," said Kenneth.

"Thank you very much, guys. I would've become an ice pick if you didn't give me that blanket," said the homeless man.

"Don't mention it. We are always glad to help another brother that's in need," said Jennifer.

"You have a nice day, and farewell. I will use this money for survival," said the homeless man.

"We will try to let this wonderful day be a blessing. Good-bye now; you take care," said Kenneth.

Surothion teleported the Thunder Warriors back to his lair since the ice storm that was created by Ravaco was so overwhelming that they had to come up with a plan.

"Thunder Warriors shouldn't be driving your cars in the middle of an ice storm that was created by Omnizar's demon," said Surothion.

"We didn't know that Omnizar had a demon on the streets that we can't even see," said Kenneth.

"You guys are going to have to do a better job of seeing clearly," said Surothion.

"Surothion, I've come up with a clever plan. I will strike the ice storm with my sword, and then you obliterate the ice beams," said Izon.

"That's an awesome plan; let's roll out now," said Surothion.

The Thunder Warriors, Izon, and Surothion went to fight Ravaco, but Ravaco wasn't going to let them win. He froze the Thunder Warriors' legs, and Surothion and Izon were the only ones fighting.

"Ravaco, you will never freeze these people to death," Supreme Lightning Blaze Surothion shouted.

"These ice fields will not remain inside this area," Ariel Sword Neutron Fury Izon shouted.

"Your attacks may have destroyed parts of me, but the Thunder Warriors won't get away," Magma Ice Beams Ravaco shouted.

"Surothion, we can't move. Our legs have been turned into ice, and there's not that much we could do," said Jennifer.

"I want all of you to stay where you are. Me and Izon will fight Ravaco," Supreme Lightning Blaze Surothion shouted.

"The two of you shall face my unmitigated fury," Magma Ice Beams Ravaco shouted.

"I specialize in the big finish," Ariel Sword Neutron Fury Izon shouted.

The attacks that came from Izon and Surothion destroyed Ravaco completely, and the Thunder Warriors' legs were restored to normal, but Omnizar would never give up. He kidnapped a young girl and put explosive radiation on her. She was very afraid the radiation explosives would trigger the mother of all black holes that exist outside of space, which would get ready to head toward earth.

"Please, let me go; I beg you. I didn't do anything wrong to anybody," said the girl.

"Silence, you human. Only I get to speak inside this dimension. I see that Surothion's going to take the bait," said Omnizar.

"Master Omnizar, I'd better go and bring the girl to earth now so the black hole will be triggered within space," said Zervo.

"Ha-ha, everything is falling into place exactly the way I wanted it to. Take the girl, and I want you to stand outside of Star Field City and then act like you are going to let her go; then press the button, and the radiation energy will activate," said Omnizar.

"It shall be done, and farewell," said Zervo.

Zervo went to earth with the kidnap victim. He stood outside of Star Field University. He knew very well that this was going to bring plenty of attention from the people who were walking by, but all of this chaos was interrupted by the Thunder Warriors.

"What are you looking at, you college punk? Pull your pants up and keep walking," said Zervo.

"I was just wondering why you have a girl tied to the ground with radiation energy explosives," said the stranger.

"Listen. It isn't your business. If you don't go now, I will use my sword to destroy you," said Zervo.

"I'm walking; peace out. Just, please, don't hurt me," said the stranger.

"That's right. You'd better run, you idiot boy," said Zervo.

"Zervo, you'd better get out of here now since there are a lot of people that are staring at you," said Randy.

"You Thunder Warriors, I knew that you were going to show up. That's why I decided to make a scene. You can have the girl. I'm out of here," said Zervo.

"That was crazy. Zervo just threw the girl at me, and he left," said Cody.

"I believe that he is behind something, but I don't know what. It doesn't sound too funny for him to let her go like that," said Larutio.

"You're right. Whoa, the clock is quickly ticking. We have to hurry up and remove the radioactive energy explosives," said Jennifer.

"I see the clock. We aren't able to remove them; they are strapped on her too hard," said Letitia.

"Everybody, just lay on the floor now; she's going to explode," yelled Zomar.

"We're too late. She already has, and I see a giant black hole coming from the sky. It's swallowing everything that is on earth. Help me, guys. I'm holding on to this flagpole, and the wind keeps pushing me toward the black hole," said Billy.

"Billy, we can't reach your arm since we are struggling to stay on the ground," said Cody.

"Dude, I am worn-out, and we can't help you out," said Jennifer.

"Hang on, guys, because we are in the fight of our lives," said Kenneth.

"Thunder Warriors, use your powers; that will create a portal, and it will keep you safe on the ground," said Surothion.

"We're doing just that, Surothion. But I'm very concerned that the black hole may injure somebody," said Larutio.

"We should use our powers to push the black hole back into space," Ariel Sword Neutron Fury Izon shouted.

"I'm positive that my attack should be enough to push the black hole away," shouted Supreme Lightning Blaze Surothion.

The attacks that came from Surothion and Izon knocked the black hole back into deep space so it wouldn't make its way toward earth and endanger the humans again. Nobody got sucked into the black hole, and the girl who had the radioactive explosives on her survived.

"Thank you very much, Surothion, for saving all of us. We owe you the world," said Suzie.

"Suzie, I'm very glad that the radioactive explosives didn't hurt you. Take care and farewell," said Surothion.

"Well, I guess the day was saved again by the infamous thunder leader," said Randy.

"You can say that. I'm just glad that nobody got killed or injured. Let's head for class now," said Zomar.

"You guys were so lucky. When I was coming to class, I saw the black hole reaching for all of you," said Professor Aaron.

"Luck isn't a word that I often use. I consider myself thankful," said Kenneth.

"That's good to hear from you. Today's lesson is about sexual harassment in the workplace; that's something very serious," said Professor Aaron.

"It happens all the time and everywhere. The police take it very seriously," said Lynx.

"But everyone has to understand that when a female doesn't get the job that she wants, she sues the employer, and that is where she messes up," said Professor Aaron.

"The last person who sexually harassed a woman got six years in prison; that is a serious sentence," said Letitia.

"You guys haven't gotten the whole point of what I'm trying to say. Everyone must respect each other in the workplace regardless of their ethnicity," said Cody.

"We know that there are a lot of perverts in the workplace, and that is why behaving properly is something that should be done all the time. The lesson is over, and everyone can close their books up. Next time we will have a math quiz, and all of you should be prepared," said Professor Aaron.

After the lesson ended, the Thunder Warriors left. They were getting ready to go home, but Surothion wouldn't let that happen; he teleported them to his lair. They were going to learn about Dead Sea coins, and Surothion was going to send them to Egypt in order to find the sea coins.

"I know that I interrupted all of you when you were getting ready to head home, but we've got some serious problems on our hands. Omnizar is after the Dead Sea coins. They represent the four deadly skull soldiers that were locked away because they sought to destroy the earth and everything that existed," said Surothion.

"Whoa, I've always heard about sea scrolls, but the Dead Sea coins are new to me," said Kenneth.

"Surothion, we don't even know where they are. You may want to tell us the actual location of these coins," said Cody.

"The Dead Sea coins are in Egypt. You will be going by yourselves. I don't want Izon to assist you in anything as of right now," said Surothion.

"Surothion, the Thunder Warriors need me so they don't have a hard time," said Izon.

"Izon, I want to see how the Thunder Warriors are when neither of us are with them as they go on their quest," said Surothion.

"I suppose you are correct, so I will just stay put for now," said Izon.

"I feel so nervous that we won't make it alive out of Egypt," said Randy.

"Dude, you need to stop being so afraid. We are with you in this one, and nothing bad will happen," said Larutio.

"I'm teleporting you guys there now. Take care, and see you later," said Surothion.

Surothion teleported the Thunder Warriors to the caves of Egypt. They saw that it was very dark in the caves, so they had to use their thunder powers to light up torches in the caves. They knew trouble was getting ready to take place when Zervo appeared with a group of vampire demons.

"I'm so confused right now. Look, the cave is so long that we don't even know how far it will take us," said Jennifer.

"Everybody, you have to get on the ground because these arrows are coming at us," said Zomar.

"Thanks a lot for saving us all. We didn't even see those arrows since they were invisible," said Letitia.

"Hey, you Thunder Warriors shouldn't be in these caves; the Dead Sea coins belong to Master Omnizar," said Zervo.

"Zervo, you've got no business following us. We're just doing the job that Surothion sent us to do," said Cody.

"I'm not following you; you're just getting in my way. Destroy them, vampire demons," said Zervo.

"We see that you thunder punks come in packs, so I'll do this," Obliteration Gate Vampiraso shouted.

"We can't use our powers since they have us trapped and tied within a gate," said Randy.

"Ha-ha, you Thunder Warriors lose, and the Dead Sea coins will go to Master Omnizar. Good-bye," said Zervo.

"Surothion is going to be very upset with us, guys. We couldn't even get the Dead Sea coins by ourselves," said Billy.

"Zervo is faster than us, and we couldn't do nothing. Let's go," said Randy.

When the Thunder Warriors failed to get the Dead Sea coins, this angered Surothion greatly, so he yelled at them, and they weren't very happy about it at all.

"You see, Surothion, I should've gone with them, but you insisted they must go on their own," said Izon.

"I find this to be very ridiculous. I sent all of you to get those Dead Sea coins, and it's very sad that Zervo is always ahead of you," said Surothion.

"Look, it's not our fault, and you shouldn't be yelling at us like this. Zervo had some serious help, and we weren't able to defend ourselves," said Kenneth.

"Maybe all of you aren't cut out to be the Thunder Warriors since you lose most of the time," said Surothion.

"Excuse you. We are just at the beginning of our journey. Besides, we're not giving up on becoming heroes of earth," said Jennifer.

"Hold on, guys. We need to take a break for a couple of days from saving the earth," said Billy.

"It sounds to me like you guys are quitters," said Izon.

"That's not what we're saying, Izon; we just have to relax our minds," said Cody.

"I'm sorry for yelling at you guys, but sometimes I must be hard on all of you. When you make a mistake. it will affect all of us," said Surothion.

After the Thunder Warriors left Surothion's lair, each and every one of them went home. Omnizar was getting ready to summon his next demon. He was very proud of Zervo for getting the Dead Sea coins, and this had a twist.

"Job well done, Zervo. I knew you could do it," said Omnizar.

"Master Omnizar, guess what. Those Thunder Warriors showed up, and the vampire demons took care of them," said Zervo.

"Surothion has failed to remember that the evil he is trying to keep away will always be alive. I summon Zatrigliao to come forth," said Omnizar.

"Master Omnizar, those Thunder Warriors won't exist any longer once I destroy them," said Zatrigliao.

"Here, take the Dead Sea coins and throw them in the air, and the skull soldiers will be released," said Omnizar.

"Your request shall be fulfilled. Farewell," said Zatrigliao.

Zatrigliao headed for earth. Once he arrived there, he threw the four Dead Sea coins in the sky, the sunlight reflected off them, and the skull soldiers came forth. Then Zatrigliao turned the earth into a volcanic forest. Massive lava began to destroy Star Field City, and the skull soldiers used their aerial obliteration beams to destroy the earth. Surothion and the Thunder Warriors went to fight Zatrigliao and the skull soldiers.

"Guys, I wouldn't want to get burned by the volcano fire that we see," said Larutio.

"Come on. Don't worry about the volcano fire. It won't hurt any of you, so attack now," Supreme Lightning Blaze Surothion shouted.

"As you can see, I've got some reinforcements, so attack while you can and be destroyed. Oh no, your attack has destroyed some of my volcanoes," said Zatrigliao.

"Ravcon lightning," shouted Jennifer.

"Zirconium lightning," shouted Kenneth.

"Mercury lightning, shouted Randy.

"All of you can attack us as much as you want, but your attacks won't have any effect," Magnetic Fury Skulatris shouted.

"The Thunder Warriors have been turned into stone, Izon. I guess this battle is us versus Zatrigliao and the skull soldiers," said Surothion.

"Surothion, I'm going to get rid of Zatrigliao's volcanoes starting now," Ariel Sword Neutron Fury Izon shouted.

"You skull soldiers are powerful—I will give you that—but your powers aren't mightier than mine," Supreme Lightning Blaze Surothion shouted.

"Those are bold words coming from the powerful thunder leader. We will turn your attacks into firecrackers," said Skulisato.

"Izon, I don't understand what is going on. Our attacks aren't working at all. What should we do?" said Surothion.

"Surothion, I know that we've never done this before, but you should fuse with me," said Izon.

"But how is that possible since we don't have an energy source?" asked Surothion.

"Whoa, check this out. Something inside your pocket is glowing," said Izon.

"Unbelievable. I'm shocked that the moonstones are back since they were destroyed last time," said Surothion.

"Listen to me, Surothion. activate your thunder fusion now," said Izon.

"Right; I'm on it. Thunder fusion, activate," said Surothion.

When Surothion fused with Izon, they became Thunder Dragon Knight, but Surothion learned a secret: Izon had a human identity when they fused.

"Zatrigliao, your end is approaching, and so is yours, you two skull soldiers," said Thunder Dragon Knight.

"So the two of you decided to fuse. This should be interesting," Zatriglato Destroyer Zatrigliao shouted.

"Oh, please, don't make us laugh with your silly attack," said Thunder Dragon Knight.

"It can't be possible my attack didn't work," said Zatrigliao.

"I told you that I'm not like any force you've ever fought," Thunder Izlaton Fury Thunder Dragon Knight shouted.

"Megrion nitro," shouted Skulisato.

"Trabicklacu fury," shouted Skulatris.

"Niteroi destroyer," shouted Skullinko.

"Impezrku obliteration," shouted Skulako.

The attack that came from Thunder Dragon Knight destroyed the skull soldiers and Zatrigliao, and the earth was restored back to normal. Izon and Surothion defused themselves. The Thunder Warriors were very happy that life was back to being regular for them, so they went to the beach since it was a nice sunny day.

"I'm so happy that we are at the beach having fun," said Kenneth.

"Dude, I am going to create a lightning surfboard so I can surf on the ocean waters," said Billy.

"I don't recommend you do that. What if you fall and drown or the sharks eat you alive?" asked Randy.

"Come on. You don't know what you are talking about. I'm not going to drown; it's completely normal," said Billy.

"Go ahead, buddy; we're not stopping you at all," said Larutio.

"Check me out, guys. I'm surfing through the sky, and we're all flying up high…. Whoa, I'm losing control of my thunder powers," said Billy.

"Billy, are you all right? Help Cody before he drowns; I see a shark behind him," said Zomar.

"I've got this one, dude. Billy, you need to listen to Randy when he tells you something," said Cody.

"I will. I guess I shouldn't try to be hardheaded by not following directions," said Billy.

"You should just use a regular surfboard instead of using your powers," said Cody.

"I hope Randy can forgive me, and peace out," said Billy.

The Thunder Warriors finished their trip to the beach. They all went home. But they were about to get into some deep trouble when they got caught up in a spider's web as they were going to Surothion's lair in the forest.

"Ay, will you guys just pull me out of this damn spiderweb?" said Jennifer.

"Hey, I'm trapped too. Surothion, you'd better get out here now and help us," shouted Letitia.

"Okay, I'm here. You guys could've teleported instead of walking through these bushes," said Surothion.

"The teleporting thing doesn't work all the time," said Randy.

"I'm deeply sorry. We're out of here now," said Surothion.

"So, is that much better for all of you now?" asked Izon.

"I'm all right since things have gone quite uphill," said Cody.

"I understand that this was supposed to be a day of fun for all of you, but I'm sorry. Sometimes you must work harder. We've got an emergency on our hands: the dragon brotherhood have set foot upon Star Field City," said Surothion.

"Are these dragon brotherhoods monsters that terrorize people?" asked Larutio.

"I'm afraid to tell you guys that this has deeply affected me. The dragon brotherhood has escaped from the underworld, and it is up to us to stop them since the dragon brotherhood possess incredible power," said Surothion.

"The only thing we've got to say is watch your back and look out for each other," said Izon.

"We will, Izon, and take care," said Larutio.

"Don't leave just yet; I'm coming with all of you," said Surothion.

The Thunder Warriors and Surothion went to Star Field City. They were getting ready to fight the dragon brotherhood, which had diabolical plans that involved burning the warriors with fire and turning them into metal.

"Well, if it isn't the Thunder Warriors and Surothion. You cowards should hiding behind trees," shouted Dragoton.

"We will never be afraid of you," Surenolize Thunder Jennifer shouted.

"Proton lightning," shouted Randy.

"Mercury lightning," shouted Cody.

"Solar flare lightning," shouted Larutio.

"Astro lightning," shouted Zomar.

"Supreme lightning blaze," shouted Surothion.

"Ha-ha, you weakling thunder bums, your attacks only reenergized us," Dragon Blaze Nitro Dragnovos shouted.

"Izon, are you watching any of this? The attack that came from Dragnovos turned the Thunder Warriors into metal," said Surothion.

"Surothion, we might have to pull back since the god of thunder hasn't come yet," said Izon.

"I'm guessing that you are talking about Prometheus, who was locked away forever," said Surothion.

"You dragon brotherhoods have won this battle, but I guarantee you that we will return and this fight won't be the same as it is now. Farwell," said Izon.

Surothion and Izon left the fight. They were going to search for Prometheus, but it wouldn't be simple. In order to release Prometheus, you must have the lightning sword and insert it into the mountain floor of Minnesota, so they went to find the lightning sword in the mountains. Omnizar wouldn't let them get that easily, so he sent his shadow vampires to attack them.

"Who knew that the mountains would have these bushes covering them?" said Surothion.

"Surothion, what can you expect? The mountains are far away, and you must walk to get there," said Izon.

"Surothion, you and Izon better walk now and return to your lair because the thunder sword belongs to Master Omnizar," said Heto.

"Omnizar is such a nerve-racking time bomb. He doesn't know when to quit," Supreme Lightning Blaze Surothion shouted.

"Hold it right there. I will counter your attack," Shadow Nister Vampiraso shouted.

"I am stepping in to help get rid of you all," Ariel Sword Neutron Fury Izon shouted.

"Nice work, Izon. Our attacks obliterated those shadow vampires," said Surothion.

"I'm here to bail you out, buddy. Whoa, I see a glowing light in between those trees," said Izon.

"Could it be the thunder sword that we were looking for?" asked Surothion.

"No, it's just a damn frog that's glowing its tail at us," said Izon.

"I'm picking up a huge signal, and it's coming from that rock over there," said Surothion.

"Hang on, buddy. I see the sword. We've got to pull it out now," Ariel Sword Neutron Fury Izon shouted.

"This is awesome. We did it, and the sword is ours," said Surothion.

"Wait. The thunder sword is shining its light, and I believe we must find the thunder symbol in the ground so we can insert the sword for the coming of Prometheus," said Izon.

Surothion and Izon continued to walk at the end of the mountain until they found the thunder symbol in the ground. They were very lucky Izon saw the symbol. They inserted the sword into the ground.

"Oh, I am positively certain that we found what we were looking for," said Surothion.

"I see the direct ground. By the powers of the thunder defenders, we call upon Prometheus, the god of thunder, to come forth," said Izon.

"I see that someone has awakened me and there is trouble in the town," said Prometheus.

"We need your help. The dragon brotherhood are causing chaos upon Star Field City, and you must help us destroy them," said Surothion.

"Did you say the dragon brotherhood? I helped defeat them; I don't know how they were able to escape from the underworld," said Prometheus.

"I suppose we are headed back to the battlefield for the ultimate fight," said Izon.

"It's time for action, and we are going now," said Prometheus.

Izon and Surothion returned to fight the dragon brotherhood with Prometheus. The dragon brotherhood would come to learn that they were no match for Prometheus. Lightning storms were hovering all over Star Field City as the biggest battle ever would take place.

"Surothion, ha-ha, so you've returned on your own to fight us, huh?" asked Dragotis.

"I'm obviously not by myself. Look around. I've got someone with me," said Surothion.

"Ay, that's Prometheus, the lightning god. But it doesn't matter; he'll be destroyed too," Dragerato Fury Dragotis shouted.

"Dragotis, your attack isn't going to get you out of this one," Lightning Obliteration Rod Prometheus shouted.

"You've destroyed Dragotis, and it's my turn to give you some of my wrath," Argonon Destroyer Dragoton shouted.

"So I'm guessing you shall be the second one to go," Lightning Obliteration Rod Prometheus shouted.

"I wish that we could just watch Prometheus fight all day; he is obliterating those dragon brotherhood punks," said Izon.

"I absolutely agree with you. Besides, me and you don't have to fight; we can just sit down and relax," said Surothion.

"I refuse to stand here and watch you destroy all of us. I'm the third one to give you a piece of me," Drago Obliterator Dragnovos shouted.

"A coward like you doesn't get to be more infamous than me," Lightning Obliteration Rod Prometheus shouted.

"It feels totally cool to be free and not a metal statue," said Kenneth.

"I could've sworn that we were goners," said Billy.

"Now that you Thunder Warriors are back, I'd like to introduce you to an ally. This is Prometheus, the god of thunder," said Surothion.

"He is huge. We wouldn't have ever been able to return if it wasn't for the help of Prometheus," said Cody.

"Do not panic, Thunder Warriors. I am happy to come to your defense. If you ever have an enemy that you can't beat, just call my name, and I will appear. Farewell," said Prometheus.

"As all of you can see, that is the boss who is over me and Izon; he is more powerful than we are," said Surothion.

"You have just convinced me that fighting harder will be what we do from now on," said Larutio.

"I guess I've inspired all of you guys. Just remember one thing: the boss is watching. Peace out, and enjoy your day," said Surothion.

After Prometheus destroyed the dragon brotherhood, he left. The Thunder Warriors were very happy that they could breathe again. Surothion returned to his lair, and the Thunder Warriors went to school so they could continue their classes.

"I haven't seen you guys in days now," said Professor Aaron.

"The city was attacked by dragon monsters, who wiped us out, but someone was able to bring us back to life," said Jennifer.

"I surely don't believe your crazy story, but hey, I will just teach the class now, which is about how window glass is made," said Professor Aaron.

"That's easy. Window glass is made from fiber, which may take a while to create," said Lynx.

"Correct, but fiber could also be used to create car windows that are breakproof, so a person could avoid having damage done to their car," said Billy.

"You guys must understand that fiber could also be used for different products, such as television screens," said Professor Aaron.

"Professor Aaron, some people try to use drinking cups made out of fiber to smash in a person's head," said Larutio.

"I strongly don't recommend anybody causing each other bodily harm with a deadly weapon," said Professor Aaron.

"Glass fibers are made by skilled craftsmen; it takes years of hard work to become skilled," said Letitia.

"I'm hoping that all of you have learned that having glass windows is very important. If you don't, then your house will be very cold during the wintertime. Glass fiber can be used for all different types of things. Class is over now, and everyone can go home," said Professor Aaron.

After the lesson ended, the Thunder Warriors were on their way home. They saw a car accident take place, and Kenneth stopped his car so he could save the lady who was inside.

"Dude, you need to stop your car for a couple of minutes. There is a lady trapped inside that car accident," said Jennifer.

"I'm doing that now," said Kenneth.

He and Jennifer walked over to the car, and Kenneth said, "Are you all right, ma'am?"

"Please get me out of the car since there is a lot of oil leaking from it and I'm afraid of an explosion," said the lady.

"We are trying our hardest to pull you out. Your foot is stuck in between the seats," said Cody.

"Zomar, keep pulling her harder, and watch out for her two knees," said Randy.

A few minutes later, the lady said, "Thanks a lot for getting me out of my car; I could've died."

"At least we were able to save the day. Just stay put, and the ambulance will come in a couple of minutes," said Larutio.

After the Thunder Warriors finished saving the lady from the car accident, they went home. Meanwhile, Omnizar was getting ready to summon his next demon, but he went into a fit of rage.

"Zervo, those Thunder Warriors have infuriated me; Prometheus destroyed the dragon brotherhood," said Omnizar.

"Master Omnizar, you have to learn discipline, which can lead to great victory; you must try to not let your enemy mess with your head," said Zervo.

"You're right. I summon Riglotar to come forth," said Omnizar.

"Master Omnizar, I will take great honor in the destruction of humankind," said Riglotar.

"You'd better not disappoint me, or you'll suffer the consequences of a devastating result," said Omnizar.

"I won't, and farewell. You take care," said Riglotar.

Riglotar went to earth. Once he arrived there, he began to scatter wax ooze all throughout Star Field City. The people became giant wax candles that were destroying the earth. These wax monsters caused the people to be trapped inside their homes; they weren't able to get out. The Thunder Warriors were playing PlayStation2 at Billy's house.

"Dude, I'm going to kick your butt and cause you to crash your racing car inside the crash banicle racing competition game," said Randy.

"That will never happen; I'm already far ahead of you," said Cody.

"Guys, I need you to stop playing your video games. There's something going on outside," said Jennifer.

"Oh, no, not now. Surothion is teleporting us to his lair," said Kenneth.

"Maybe he will give us some answers since we don't know too much," said Zomar.

"All right, you guys, the wax demon is outside causing destruction, and we have to find Riglotar," said Surothion.

"When we were at the house, we saw these wax figures attacking people's windows," said Larutio.

"The only way to get rid of these wax monsters is to turn them back into the humans they were," said Zomar.

The Thunder Warriors and Surothion left his lair with Izon. They went to fight Riglotar, but it wouldn't be easy for them; Izon came to help out, and they were honored and grateful to have an extra helping hand.

"I see that we've got a lot of wax monsters looking at us, and I believe that this fight won't be simple for us," Thunder Striker Kenneth shouted.

"Ravcon lightning," shouted Jennifer.

"Mercury lightning," shouted Billy.

"Proton lightning," shouted Cody.

"Astro lightning," shouted Zomar.

"Zarteco lightning fury," shouted Larutio.

"Supreme lightning blaze," shouted Surothion.

"Izarion fury," shouted Izon.

"This is not fair. I was supposed to remain invisible, but you thunder brats unveiled me and you've destroyed my wax monsters by restoring them as humans," said Riglotar.

"You can't stay hidden any longer. Besides, it's over," Supreme Lightning Blaze Surothion shouted.

"Ay, you blew my energy candles into the air, and my power is decreasing," said Riglotar.

"That's because the wax monsters are gone, and now we will do the finish," Thunder Maze Billy shouted.

"Since all of you are going to outnumber me, then take this," Asterio Fury Riglotar shouted.

"Stand back. I've got this one," Ariel Sword Neutron Fury Izon shouted.

The attacks that came from Izon, Surothion, and the Thunder Warriors destroyed Riglotar, and the earth was back to normal.

Then the Thunder Warriors went to a scrap metal factory. They were learning what the metal was used for, and they would learn some interesting stuff.

"Do people always use jewelry for everything out there?" said Larutio.

"Not really. Our scrap metal comes from necklaces, watches, and bracelets, plus diamond rings," said Lacey.

"Wow, that's a lot of silver and gold. Do you pay your customers cash for gold buyers?" asked Cody.

"We've got hundreds of thousands of clients, including the government, which uses gold to collect their tax dollars from every department that you see," said Lacey.

"I wish that you guys could've been more realistic with us before coming here," said Jennifer.

"I was; we told you all of the truth that was needed to be told," said Letitia.

"I see that you guys are staring at all of these gold bricks and your eyes are shining like glitter," said Lacey.

"Well, we were just watching the precious metals that you've got, and I'll admit that I'm impressed by just looking at them," said Larutio.

After the Thunder Warriors finished visiting the metals factory, they planned to go home, but as they were getting ready to drive home, Omnizar appeared. He unleashed a fog that made the Thunder Warriors and everyone in Star Field City blind. Surothion quickly brought them to his lair.

"Our trip to the metals factory was not so interesting. All you saw was metals and people driving trucks with metals," said Randy.

"Dude, sometimes you're lost in your imagination. Curse you, sucker! They're supposed to be driving trucks since that is part of their job," said Cody.

"It wasn't necessary for you to be screaming in my ears like that," said Randy.

"I'm so scared, right? Omnizar is staring you dead in the eye, and he has unleashed some kind of fog and I can't see," said Jennifer.

"You're not the only one. I'm unable to open my eyes," said Zomar.

"I don't know what made you Thunder Warriors think that I wouldn't trap you and seek vengeance. Ha-ha," said Omnizar.

"I swear that your evil laugh will be the last thing that comes out of your mouth," said Billy.

"Oh, please, your threats only make me want to throw water in your face. Farewell," said Omnizar.

"Are you guys all right? I'm taking all of you back to my lair now," said Surothion.

"Surothion, we don't have our sight, and Omnizar is wickedly bad," said Jennifer.

"You guys are going to have to remain in your seats because it will take some time before your sight returns," said Surothion.

"But, Surothion, take us home so we could be with our families; maybe they will take care of us," said Larutio.

"I can't do any of that, as now you being in my lair keeps you out of harm's sight," said Surothion.

"All right then, I'm going to sleep. See you later," said Letitia.

"Ay, man, I guess Letitia was too anxious about turning invisible and sleeping in her chair," said Surothion.

The Thunder Warriors continued to stay at Surothion's lair since they could not see. Omnizar had removed their when he was getting ready to summon his next demon.

"Zervo, as you can see, those Thunder Warriors are out of the way for now, and there is no one to save Star Field City except Surothion and Izon," said Omnizar.

"Master Omnizar, you were such a genius in taking them out, but now use all the rest of the wrath you've got," said Zervo.

"Except for this time, my wrath will have a devastating effect. I summon Artenocu to come forth," said Omnizar.

"I shall take great pride in obliterating those Thunder Warriors and humans. Farewell," said Artenocu.

Artenocu went to earth. Once he arrived there, he began to use his Arknon waves. Giant acid rainstorms were devouring the earth and destroying the humans. Surothion and Izon both went to fight Artenocu.

"Izon, we're going to have to bring down these acid rains so they don't wipe out our powers," said Surothion.

"The waves are what's making Artenocu stronger, and I'm going to blow them away," Supreme Lightning Blaze Surothion shouted.

"Surothion, your attack will never stop my acid rain since it is falling ten times faster than you thought," said Artenocu.

"We call upon Prometheus, the thunder god, to come forth," said Surothion.

"Surothion, you called me at the correct time," said Prometheus.

"We need your help to destroy this acid rain and restore the Thunder Warriors' vision," said Surothion.

"Your wish shall be my command," Lightning Obliteration Rod Prometheus shouted.

"The god of thunder shall never get rid of my acid rains," Imperatu Rizio Artenocu shouted.

The attack that came from Prometheus was so devastating that it obliterated Artenocu. The Thunder Warriors were able to get their vision back since Prometheus restored it back to normal. Everybody else also got their vision back, and they all celebrated then.

"It absolutely feels great to see again; I could walk through the park singing loudly," said Kenneth.

"Well, I'm certain that Omnizar will be mad as hell that our vision has been restored," said Billy.

"I'm very happy to see that all of you are energized and excited," said Surothion.

"Surothion, you should be out there doing work like we do," said Zomar.

"I really don't do that much. My job is to keep everybody safe," said Surothion.

"I suppose that we're leaving now; farewell," said Cody.

"See you guys later on, and have a great afternoon," said Surothion.

The Thunder Warriors left Surothion's lair and went home to rest. But evil would never let Star Field City have peace. Omnizar sent Zervo to find the shadow tubes, which contained fusion demons that were imprisoned because they could turn anything into ashes with one touch.

"Vampiraso, do you see any of the shadow tubes around here?" asked Zervo.

"Zervo, the tubes are hidden within the top of the lotus vine branch, and I can't reach them since they are too high," said Vampiraso.

"I thought that you were tall, like Izon, to get up there, but I guess I was wrong," said Zervo.

"I just came up with something. If I use my powers to cut the vine branch, maybe that will work," said Vampiraso.

"You idiot! Do not do such a thing, because the vines will knock us out of these woods," said Zervo.

"I'm turning around and going to Master Omnizar to tell him that you didn't do your duties like you were supposed to," said Vampiraso.

"So, I see that you were planning to get me into trouble. Take this," Magnum Solar Strike Zervo shouted.

"Ay, you blasted me to the ground. I should just give you a piece of me," said Vampiraso.

"The two of you need to stop this silly fighting. It isn't going to work for none of us," said Vanis.

"My bad. I guess we got out of control, and it didn't work out," said Vampiraso.

"Stop for a minute. The tubes are activating, and the fusion demons are being released," said Zervo.

"Hello, Zervo. I'm guessing that it was Master Omnizar that sent you to release us," said Vocotar.

"You're right. Master Omnizar will be happy to know that the two of you are free," said Zervo.

"You need to take a closer look of where you're at. These aren't the woods," said Viriculo.

"Oh, I see it now; we are at the bottom of the earth," said Zervo.

After Zervo found the fusion demons, he left and returned to Omnizar's lair. The fusion demons went to attack the earth. They began to use their fusion solars. This attack caused the earth to rapidly disappear and vanish into space, and the life that existed was being wiped out.

The Thunder Warriors were going to do a cancer test when they teleported back to Surothion's lair.

"I'm hoping that this test comes back negative because I don't smoke or drink," said Kenneth.

"You obviously don't have to worry about it; we should all be good," said Billy.

"A vision has just popped up in my head. We'd better go now before those innocent souls are completely gone," said Randy.

"All of you did a great job by returning to my lair. The fusion demons have escaped from their imprisonment tubes, and we're fighting a force that can defeat all of us," said Surothion.

"I was suggesting that you go and fight the fusion demons by yourself," said Cody.

"Hey, don't you ever say that to me. Besides, we are all a team. If you're a punk, then run home to Mommy; this is not for you," said Surothion.

"Don't listen to him, Surothion. I guess he's just having a day where someone is down low," said Jennifer.

"I know his brain isn't being wired properly," said Surothion.

Surothion and the Thunder Warriors went to fight the fusion demons. After all, Surothion had never lost a battle.

"Oh, you Thunder Warriors, I'm guessing that all of you have come to rescue the failing and destroyed earth. Ha-ha," said Vocotar.

"The earth will never be destroyed as long as we exist," said Billy.

"Well, that's too bad. Your destruction shall be first, Argozon Fury Viriculo shouted.

"Ravcon lightning," shouted Jennifer.

"Proton lightning," shouted Kenneth.

"Mercury lightning," shouted Zomar.

"Astro lightning fury," shouted Randy.

"Supreme lightning blaze," shouted Surothion.

"Solar lightning fury," shouted Larutio.

"Magnum lightning obliterator," shouted Billy.

"We should give all of you applause. Nice try, but you've activated our fusion wormhole. This attack reflects all of your attacks back at all of you and you become stone," said Vocotar.

"Thunder Warriors, I tried, but I guess it wasn't enough," said Surothion.

"Surothion, no, we all have lost this fight, and our bodies have turned into stone," said Larutio.

"Good–bye, thunder chumps. All of you will remain stone forever. Ha-ha," said Viriculo.

"The Thunder Warriors and Surothion may be gone, but don't forget about me," said Prometheus.

"Prometheus, you should be annihilated just like they were," Varickio Destroyer Vocotar shouted.

"The two of you are like raccoons inside a pothole," Lightning Obliteration Rod Prometheus shouted.

"Vocotar, you should be safe; I've got you covered," Argozon Fury Viriculo shouted.

The attack that came from Prometheus destroyed the two fusion demons, and the earth was restored back to normal. So were the Thunder Warriors, including Surothion. Then Prometheus left.

The Thunder Warriors went to school, but the lesson that they would be given would be out of this world.

"Every time I look at you, Jennifer, you put a wonderful smile on my face," said Professor Aaron.

"Oh, thank you, I never knew that I would light up the class by just walking in," said Jennifer.

"Today's lesson is about the moon crashing into the earth," said Professor Aaron.

"I couldn't begin to imagine if the moon knocked the earth thirty-five miles into space; then we all might have been obliterated," said Lynx.

"We wouldn't be wiped out yet due to the black hole that destroys all existing life," said Billy.

"The lesson reminds me of this movie I saw called *Dark Space*. It shows you completely what would happen to earth if it got closer to the sun."

"That sounds very deep to me. I certainly would not want to become fried chicken at all," said Zomar.

"I'm showing all of you the things that take place in space. The asteroids and stars, including the moon, align altogether, but every burning star that comes from space will show you a sign of the oracle alignment," said Professor Aaron.

"Whoa, I never knew anything about this oracle alignment. Why won't you explain it to me?" asked Marcos.

"The oracle alignment is when the stars and asteroids combine to form these giant crystals that crash into the earth. Each crystal has an animal symbol on it," said Professor Aaron.

"I totally dig this lesson. It sounds very natural and cool to me," said Yanisia.

"Zomar, we would like you to read for us from page 114," said Professor Aaron.

"Most people try to steal these crystals once they crash into the earth, but they fuse to form the animal symbol. This could be a good sign of luck that occurs every year," said Zomar.

"Thank you very much. Everybody can close their books. The lesson will end here. If any of you find one of these crystals, bring it to me so I could add it to my collection. Farewell," said Professor Aaron.

After the Thunder Warriors left school, they went back to Surothion's lair because the phoenix crystals were discovered; but in order for them to get the phoenix crystals, they will have to form a circle.

"If all of you were wondering, the news I've got today is very exciting. I have found the phoenix crystals," said Surothion.

"This is awesome. I want to see them now," said Cody.

"Before we get the crystals, we must form a circle," said Surothion.

"So you mean to tell us that the phoenix crystals are in our possession?" asked Larutio.

"The only way for us to get those crystals is for us to unite as one," said Surothion.

"I'm with you, Surothion. As you can clearly see, the circle has been formed," said Jennifer.

"By the powers of the ancient thunder guardians, I call upon the phoenix crystals to come forth," said Surothion.

"Wow, that was very impressive. The phoenix crystals came out of a portal, and they are in our hands," said Billy.

"I suppose this is it. We are going to face Omnizar and Zervo for the final battle," said Surothion.

"I've learned a whole lot on this journey so that we will never bow down to evil," said Kenneth.

Omnizar knew that the Thunder Warriors had gotten the phoenix crystals. He was getting ready to face them for a final interesting fight. He left his lair with Zervo, but this fight would end with the destruction of both Omnizar and Zervo.

"Zervo, this is absolutely insane. The Thunder Warriors have the phoenix crystals," said Omnizar.

"Well then, Master Omnizar, we're going to give them a final fight that will lead to their destruction," said Zervo.

Omnizar left his lair, and so did Zervo. They went to fight the Thunder Warriors, but this wasn't going to be an ordinary fight. Omnizar began to use his vanquishing seal to destroy the humans that existed, and the Thunder Warriors used the powers of the phoenix crystals so they could summon the Fire Phoenix Thunder Dragon to fight Omnizar and Zervo.

"No way Omnizar is using his dark seal to vanquish and wipe out human souls," said Billy.

"Listen to me, Thunder Warriors. If you dare to come and fight me, you'll be obliterated just like these humans," said Omnizar.

"Omnizar, it's you who should be worried by the powers of the phoenix crystals. We call upon the Fire Phoenix Thunder Dragon to come forth," said Surothion.

"This is awesome. The Fire Phoenix Thunder Dragon is navy blue lightning. Destroy Omnizar and Zervo," said Randy.

"Damn, I can't look at the Fire Phoenix Thunder Dragon. It's destroying Omnizar and Zervo, and they can't fight back," said Cody.

"Oh no, I will get you Thunder Warriors for this once I return from hell," said Omnizar.

"Omnizar, you'll never be coming back. Once the Fire Phoenix Thunder Dragon destroys you, it's permanent," said Surothion.

"Uh, the fire, it's burning me as I'm being annihilated by the Fire Phoenix Thunder Dragon," screamed Omnizar.

The Fire Phoenix Thunder Dragon destroyed Omnizar and Zervo, and the earth was restored back to normal. The Thunder Warriors forgot that their journey wasn't over yet, because next year they would be fighting a new evil force. The battle to defend the earth wasn't over yet since dark forces continued and wanted to wipe out humankind. That is why the Thunder Warriors were there to protect the universe and the humans that lived on the earth. So, the fight would continue.

But the Thunder Warriors got a shocking surprise: Zervo was back. He was now teaming up with Lavatoriax, and this meant plenty of trouble for the Thunder Warriors. They did not bother to panic nor be afraid, as Surothion was getting ready for the next part of his journey. He knew that things weren't going quite the way he expected them to since the Thunder Warriors laughed and joked about him, but he chose to let it go, not pay any attention to them, and keep it moving.

The eight Thunder Warriors were getting ready for their second year of college.

About the Author

My main goal is to be a fully established mainstream writer. It changed my life to become an inspiration to other people, and I want to help change lives and help people who are in need.

Printed in the United States
By Bookmasters